RESCUE

MARIE ETCHELL

Red Deer Press

Published in the United States in 2023

Published in Canada by Red Deer Press, 209 Wicksteed Avenue, Unit 51, Toronto, ON M4G 0B1

Published in the United States by Red Deer Press, 311 Washington Street, Brighton, MA 02135

Library and Archives Canada Cataloguing in Publication
Title: Rescue / by Marie Etchell.
Names: Etchell, Marie, author.
Identifiers: Canadiana 20210394021 | ISBN 9780889956650 (softcover)
Subjects: LCGFT: Novels.
Classification: LCC PS8609.T33 R47 2022 | DDC jC813/.6—dc23

Publisher Cataloging-in-Publication Data (U.S.)
Names: Etchell, Marie, author.
Title: Rescue / Marie Etchell.
Description: Markham, Ontario : Red Deer Press, 2022.| Summary: "Charlie Campbell is twelve
and his life is in tatters: his parents are splitting, he's quit soccer, he hasn't had a growth spurt yet
and he wants a dog more than anything. He hatches a plan to volunteer at the vet's and prove to
his mom that he can be responsible"-- Provided by publisher.
Identifiers: ISBN 978-0-88995-665-0 (paperback)
Subjects: LCSH Parents — Juvenile fiction. | Veterinarians -- Juvenile fiction. | Volunteers --
Juvenile fiction. | Resilience – Juvenile fiction. | BISAC: JUVENILE FICTION / Social Themes /
Emotions & Feeling. | JUVENILE FICTION / Social Themes / Self-Esteem & Self-Reliance.
Classification: LCC PZ7.1.E834Res |DDC 813.6 – dc23

Red Deer Press acknowledges with thanks the Canada Council for the
Arts and the Ontario Arts Council for their support of our publishing program.
We acknowledge the financial support of the Government of Canada through
the Canada Book Fund (CBF) for our publishing activities.

Edited for the Press by Beverley Brenna
Text and cover design by Tanya Montini
Printed in Canada by AIIM– Avant Imaging & Integrated Media Inc.

To Adrian and Alexander

Chapter 1

THE LIST

Charlie Campbell's Qualifications for Volunteering at Dr. Anderton's Vet Clinic

1. Passionate about animals, especially dogs.
2. Live close to the clinic and can bike there.
3. Responsible and mature. (I can provide references from my soccer coach.)
4. Some people say I'm an animal whisperer. (I saved a robin that everyone said was going to die.)
5. Will work for free.
6. Not squeamish.
7. Strong and able to lift heavy things.
8. Not playing soccer this year so I'm free after school.
9. If you say yes to me, you could say no to anyone else who asks.
10. ~~My mom and dad are separating and a volunteering~~

~~job would help me to think about other things.~~

10. ~~I want a dog more than anything and if I can't have one at least this way I can be near dogs.~~

10. ~~Did I mention that I really love dogs and would love to work with them.~~

10. Don't mind the sight of blood.

"Cool," Samir said, handing the list back to Charlie. "I mean, it's cool if that's what you want to do."

Charlie sniffed in the mouth-watering smells coming from Samir's kitchen all the way down to where they sat on the front steps. He hugged his knees to his chest, unconsciously comparing the size of Samir's big feet to his own. Samir had shot up over the summer. Charlie hadn't, even though he'd be turning 13 in the winter. His feet still looked like little kids' feet.

Samir stuffed the rest of a samosa into his mouth and chewed it right down to nothing. "But I still don't get why you quit soccer. I thought you really loved it."

Charlie pulled at the frayed threads on the knees of his jeans. He didn't love anything anymore. But it was impossible to explain it to Samir, because Samir's dad wasn't about to move out, and Samir probably didn't feel like he'd fallen into a giant pit of elephant poo.

"It's complicated," Charlie said.

Chapter 2

THE CALL

Charlie scowled at the blobs of spaghetti sauce congealing in the pot, and the heap of cooking utensils piled up in the sink. It was his turn to do the dishes, but he *had* to make the call now. Mark would be home any minute from his Sunday shift at Burger Baron, and Charlie didn't want to be reminded for the millionth time that it was dumb to work for free. He wished he'd never told his older brother he was going to try to volunteer at the vet's.

He gripped the phone, his hand slippery with sweat. Dr. Anderton was a golf buddy of his dad's. Still. It was kind of nervy, calling him at home on the weekend.

He breathed in, slow and long, before picking up his list. He punched in the numbers and listened to the rings. One. Two. Three. Four.

"Hello?" a male voice answered. It was Dr. Anderton,

for sure. Charlie had only met him twice, but the voice sounded right.

He swallowed. "Hello, Dr. Anderton. It's Charlie Campbell." He waited, knocked off balance by the dead air.

"Charlie," Dr. Anderton said finally. "It took me a second to place your name. What can I do for you?"

Charlie eased himself down on the stool. His hand shook so hard he had to set the list on the counter.

He'd practiced the words, so he knew what to say, but his tongue felt like it was caught on the roof of his mouth. "Dr. Anderton," he said, "I'd like to apply for a position as a volunteer at your clinic."

He'd barely got the words out before Dr. Anderton spoke. "Oh, Charlie," he sighed. "We are such a small clinic and it's so hectic. Even though I know you, and I know your folks, and I'm sure you'd do a good job— we'd be tripping over each other."

Charlie's heart hammered out of control. Dr. Anderton was saying no. It wasn't going to happen. He wasn't going to get to work with dogs. His whole life was going to stay one big pile of poop.

"Charlie." Dr. Anderton sounded tired. "I get so

many requests from people who want to volunteer here. It's not just you. I say no to everybody."

Charlie picked up the list again, and gripped it so hard, he crumpled the bottom half of the sheet. He ran his eyes down all the reasons. Then he took a calculated risk, leaping to Number 9.

"Dr. Anderton," he said, "I understand what you're saying, but honestly, I promise I'd be the best volunteer ever. I'd do all the grunt work. I'd take out the garbage and clean the cages and wash the floor." He paused, and then practically shouted his last and most important point. "And think of it this way: if you said yes to me, you could tell anybody else who asked that you already have all the volunteers you can handle."

Charlie held his breath. In the background, he heard dishes clanking. Someone, maybe Mrs. Anderton, was doing dishes. He could relate. It was probably her turn, and she didn't like it much, either. The seconds ticked by. It was a long silence.

Dr. Anderton cleared his throat. "Charlie," he said, sighing heavily into the phone.

After that, there was silence again. Charlie wondered if they'd been disconnected.

"How strange," Dr. Anderton continued finally. He sounded disoriented, as if he'd forgotten he was talking to Charlie. "I felt ..." he paused again. "I felt ..." Then he laughed, nervously, as if he was embarrassed.

Charlie didn't know what to say. The situation was awkward.

"Charlie." Dr. Anderton's voice sounded funny. "Sometimes ..." He paused again. "Sorry, Charlie," he said. "I'm feeling a little light-headed, almost tingly."

"Oh," Charlie said, hoping Dr. Anderton was all right.

Dr. Anderton cleared his throat. "Well, yes, as I was saying, sometimes we do get overwhelmed at the clinic. Sometimes ..." he paused again. "Sometimes we get a stray or a lost dog that needs our attention. Sometimes ..." He cleared his throat again. "Yes," he said finally. "You can volunteer at the clinic. Not every day. Maybe two or three days a week. After school. And we'll have to see how it goes. If Megan says it isn't working, then we stop. Megan is my right arm, and if she's not happy, I'm not happy."

Charlie practically bit through his bottom lip, trying to keep from boiling over with excitement. In a heartbeat, he didn't feel so bad about quitting soccer, and he didn't care that Mark thought working for nothing was stupid.

He took another leap. "What do you think," he said, "if I start on Monday?"

Chapter 3

FIRST SHIFT

Charlie had meant to arrive early for his first shift, but Ms. Li had snagged him to talk about his math homework, just as he was closing his locker. Then, when he got home, Mom had made him take out the garbage, which he should have done before he went to school. Now he was running late.

It was only about five kilometres to the vet clinic from Charlie's house. Not far, especially on his new bike. Still. He was going to have to pedal fast.

He peeled out of his driveway, rode no-hands while he fastened his helmet, and then leaned in. As the dreaded Saddlehorn Hill loomed into view, he geared down and pushed harder.

He was practically gagging by the time he made it to the top. It didn't help when two gravel trucks, spewing stinky black diesel smoke, blew past him. He shifted into high gear and crouched over the handlebars, for the steep downhill before the turnoff to the clinic. The wind in his face forced tears out of his eyes. He had to be on time. It would look terrible if he showed up late for his first shift.

He was still careening at top speed, as he blew past the equestrian centre next to the clinic. He coasted the last few metres, and then skidded into the gravel driveway. He wheeled his bike around the side of the building, leaned it up against the fence, and locked it. The clinic was practically out in the country and surrounded by fields, but his bike was still pretty shiny, and there was no point taking a chance on it getting stolen. That was the thing about living on the outskirts of town. No buses. Without a bike, he'd be hooped.

Charlie walked back around to the front, butterflies summersaulting in his stomach. He lifted his hand to the door. He'd never done anything like this before. He could hardly breathe.

The cowbell over the door clanged as he stepped inside. He breathed the sharp smell of antiseptic. The waiting room was empty, and a sign on the reception desk said *I'll be right back*. A display case along one wall held jars with strange-looking contents, that Charlie thought he'd like to study more closely, when he had a chance.

A female voice called out, "Hello!" Then a door into the back flew open, and Charlie saw a girl with turquoise hair in a long ponytail, and round glasses framing her smiling green eyes. She carried a black cat that had bandages around its middle.

"Hey! You must be Charlie. I'm Dr. Anderton's receptionist, girl Friday, undocumented veterinary assistant, social coordinator, and trouble-shooter. But you can just call me Megan."

Charlie let out his breath. She was nice, and younger than she looked in her picture on the clinic web page.

"Dr. Anderton was hoping to be here when you arrived, but he got called out to deliver a foal. I'm supposed to show you around and get you started."

"Okay. Good to meet you." Charlie pulled off his helmet and ran his hands through his hair. He could tell it was sticking up in sweaty tufts.

"Come on through here," Megan said, walking ahead of him through a big open room to a hallway by the back door. "You can put your pack here, and hang your jacket and stuff on the hooks."

She waited while Charlie stowed his things, then led him back to the big open room they'd just walked through.

"You're right on time, by the way," she said. "That's good, because Dr. Anderton wants me to keep track of your hours, so he doesn't overpay you."

"But I—" Charlie stuttered.

Megan burst out laughing. "Gotcha!"

Charlie's face burned. He narrowed his eyes. Not to worry. He'd get her back when he got the hang of things around here.

"This is Blackie, by the way," Megan said, shifting the cat to one arm and scratching him under the chin. "We've just been having a little cuddle. He had a tumor removed yesterday, and he still feels pretty sorry for himself."

Charlie leaned in and gave Blackie a gentle rub around the ears. The cat opened one eye and mewed.

"So," Megan began, "let's have a quick tour." She pointed to two doors. Those are the surgery rooms, at least, in theory. In actual fact, Dr. Anderton only uses this one." She flicked a switch, and the room was flooded with brilliant light. "The other one is mainly used for storage."

She turned the lights off and pulled the door shut. "This room we've been standing in," Megan continued, "is sort of an all-purpose space. It's where Dr. A does the minor stuff, like changing bandages and giving shots and cleaning teeth."

Charlie tried to take in every detail. In the centre of the room was a large, raised bathtub, covered by a stainless-steel examining table. Two walls had cabinets with glass doors, and through the glass, he could see bottles and packages and boxes of equipment. The other two walls were lined with framed photographs.

Charlie moved to where he could look more closely. There were pictures of bulls with blue ribbons pinned to their horns, Siamese cats with mysterious blue eyes, families with beloved pets, even a photo of a rooster with a cast on one leg.

"Wow!" he said.

"Yeah," Megan agreed. "Dr. Anderton has a very busy practice. Big animal and small animal. You don't see that very often these days." She moved to the centre of the room. "See this tub area? This'll be one of your jobs. It has to be totally cleaned every time it's used. First you put on these stylish rubber gloves. Then you disinfect with this." She pointed to a plastic jug on the shelf above the tub. "And here's the bucket. You put in one inch of the disinfectant and a squirt of this soap. And then you grab a sponge out of this box and scrub."

"Right." Charlie nodded. So far so good. His confidence was returning. For sure he knew how to scrub stuff.

"And don't forget …" Megan grinned at him. "There'll be blood!" She made a ghoulish face.

Charlie tried to laugh, but it came out as a squeak.

"Mostly you'll be taking care of the animals, though. Come on out here."

She led the way through a doorway into a short hall, with kennels on either side. She opened a small cage, and gently shifted Blackie onto a folded towel. She closed the gate and checked the latch.

Most of the other kennels were empty, but two were occupied. A big Golden Retriever lifted his head, ever so slightly. On the other side and further down, a fat grey tabby curled into an even tighter ball in the back corner of a cage.

"This is Olive." Megan introduced Charlie to the Retriever. "She's a cat chaser, and the last time, she ran right into the path of a delivery truck. Poor thing."

Megan bent down and opened the kennel gate. Then

she reached in and massaged the top of the dog's head. "You can't put your hand in like this with every animal. They can be vicious when they're scared and hurt."

Megan made a kissing sound, and the dog made a limp effort to lick her hand. "But it's okay with Olive. She's feeling a little better now, and she's a sweetie."

"What's wrong with her?" Charlie asked. He couldn't see any bandages or visible signs of injury.

"She lost all her teeth." Megan's voice was mournful. "Dr. A had to fit her with dentures."

Charlie was ready this time. "Well, cheaper than orthodontia, anyway."

Megan thumped Charlie on the back. "All right! Two points for you. I can see we're going to get along just fine."

Charlie flashed her an appreciative smile.

Megan took Olive's water dish and refilled it at the sink. "Actually, she had a lot of internal bruising and a couple of cracked ribs. She's lucky. It could have been way worse."

"And what about this little guy?" Charlie peered into the cat's kennel. "He doesn't look very happy."

"That's Sam. He's faking it. He just had his toenails trimmed. Not exactly major surgery, but you'd never know it to look at him."

Charlie looked down at his own fingernails and shoved his hands into his pockets.

"Come and meet the last inmate. Just arrived this morning."

Charlie followed Megan out the back door, to where a chain-link enclosure had been built onto the back of the building. Inside the enclosure, a wooden doghouse provided protection from the elements.

Megan made the introductions. "Charlie, meet Buster. Buster, this is Charlie, the new cleaning man."

Charlie ignored the comment and knelt down in front of the kennel.

Buster was the biggest Chocolate Lab he'd ever seen. His paws were the size of Charlie's hands. His head was massive. And once he'd struggled to his feet to greet them, he stood almost as high as Charlie's waist. He tried to jam his nose through the steel mesh of the kennel.

"He sure doesn't look sick." Charlie studied the dog's white whiskers. "Old maybe, but not sick."

"He's not sick, exactly," Megan said, kneeling down beside Charlie. "He's got sore hips, and he's probably suffering from a broken heart. But he's not sick in the usual way."

Buster whined, mouth wide open, revealing teeth worn down and yellowed by age.

"That's right, isn't it, big fellow. You have a broken heart, don't you?" Megan pushed her face up close to the dog's, and puckered up for a sloppy lick, right through the mesh.

"He used to be a service dog," Megan continued. "Apparently, he's got quite the résumé of people he's helped, but for the last two years, he's been a companion dog for a very old fellow, who used to live not far from here. When the man died a few days back, the family flew in from Toronto to sort things out. They didn't know what to do with the dog, so this morning, they brought him here, and Dr. Anderton didn't have the heart to say no."

"He looks like a service dog. You can tell he's got a big heart."

"I know. I totally agree. He is the sweetest Labrador I've ever met."

"So, what's going to happen to him?"

"That's the bad part. Dr. Anderton put the word out that he has an elderly Chocolate Lab looking for a family, but if he doesn't find a home for him pretty soon, he's going to put him down. It's not fair to keep him cooped up like this."

Charlie swallowed hard. "I wish I could take him," he said. But there was no point asking Mom. He wanted a dog more than anything, but he'd already been through the pet thing a million times. Mom was allergic to dogs. And now they might have to move.

"Trouble is," Megan said, "everybody wants a puppy. All people think about, with an old dog like Buster, is the vet bills."

Charlie stifled an anguished groan. He locked eyes with the dog.

Megan stood up and brushed bits of gravel off her pants. "There is one couple Dr. Anderton knows. They've got a farm on Vancouver Island. They might be interested. They're thinking about it."

"He's perfect," Charlie said, sticking his fingers through the steel mesh, and stroking Buster's grizzled muzzle.

"Glad you like him," Megan said, as she pulled open the back door of the clinic. "He's all yours while he's here. He'll need to be walked and brushed, and fed and watered. But wait and deal with him in the last half-hour of your shift. That way, he'll be ready to get back in his kennel before we lock up for the night." She grinned. "Come on. I'll show you where the mop is."

Charlie turned to follow Megan inside, but something made him look back.

Buster was sitting on his haunches, and Charlie could see the dog's chest rising and falling. His mouth was open like he was trying to speak. His brown eyes bored into Charlie's.

Charlie's heart raced. He'd never been electrocuted, but he was positive this is what it would feel like.

Buster heaved himself back up on all fours, and shuffled to the corner of the kennel closest to Charlie. He pressed his face into the steel mesh, his eyes glowing with life. He was telling Charlie something.

Charlie shook off the sensation of an electric current running between him and Buster. "I'll be back before you know it," he whispered. It was all he could do to close the clinic door behind him.

He stopped for a moment to catch his breath. He'd already broken a cardinal rule for wannabe vets: he'd fallen in love with a patient.

Chapter 4

WALKING THE DOG

"Okay, Charlie, wash up." Megan pointed to the soap dispenser. "Two minutes. Scrub hard, and then I'll show you how to change a dressing."

Charlie scrubbed his hands with the strong-smelling soap. As he dried them, he glanced up at the clock. In one hour, he could be with Buster.

Megan opened Blackie's cage and gently eased the cat out. She set him down on his side, on the cold stainless-steel surface of the examination table. "There we go, little one," she said.

The cat mewed and stretched.

Megan handed Charlie a pair of soft leather gloves from the shelf above the table. "Just in case," she said, and waited for Charlie to pull them on. "Now, your job is to hold him steady. Easy does it. That's it. If you keep him still, that gives me two hands to remove the bandage, and we'll take a look at his incision."

Charlie watched intently, as Megan used one hand to gently pull the bandage away from the cat's shaved skin, and the other to slip the rounded tip of the scissors under the white cotton gauze.

"That's it, doing great," Megan whispered.

Charlie didn't know if the words were meant for him or for Blackie, but it didn't matter.

"Sutures look good," Megan said, clearing the bandages into the waste bin. She pointed with the scissors. "See? It all looks clean and calm. If it looks puffy or red, that's a sign of infection, and that's not good. We'll put another bandage on now, and then, by tomorrow, we'll want to let the air get at it a bit to speed the healing."

While Megan opened a new dressing, Charlie eased his grip on the cat and scratched her ears, talking in a low soft voice the way Megan had done.

"Doing great," Megan said again, and Charlie felt a rush of pride. He stole another look at the clock.

After that, the minutes flew by. Megan showed him how to hold Olive's mouth closed, and then massage her jaw, so she'd swallow her antibiotic pill. He filled water bowls and doled out lamb and rice combos. He mopped out Olive's kennel after her owners came to pick her up, and he got to answer the phone twice. He was pretty sure Megan let him do a whole lot more than Dr. Anderton might have done.

He'd lost all track of time, when Megan tapped her watch and pointed to the back door. "You better go see to Buster. His kibble's in the bin in his kennel, and he gets two cups."

Charlie grabbed the leash that hung beside the back door and slipped out.

Buster was already on his feet, vocalizing in a high-pitched whine, and wagging his tail so hard, his whole back end shook.

Charlie reached in and clipped the leash onto the loop of Buster's collar. Buster pranced with expectation, his gaze riveted on Charlie.

They started off across the parking lot behind the clinic, empty except for Megan's dusty Corolla. It was colder than when Charlie had arrived for his shift, a typical day in late October, when it could be warm at noon, but chilly later in the afternoon. He wished he'd thought to grab his jacket.

Buster led the way, stopping once to lift his leg on a

concrete barrier, once again on a pile of leaves someone had raked up, and again on the tire of a parked pickup truck. Charlie relaxed his grip on the leash. Buster seemed content to smell the flowers.

And then, Buster stopped, his right foreleg poised in midair, his nose to the wind. He strained on the leash, like he knew where he wanted to go. His shuffling gait disappeared. Charlie grasped the leash and hung on.

They sped to the back of the lot, past a couple of rusty vehicles with weeds growing out of their bumpers, and into the unfenced field behind the clinic. Buster broke into a run and pounded ahead, his tongue hanging out and drool flying. He seemed to have forgotten Charlie, clinging to the end of the leash.

Charlie kept his eyes on the ground. The late afternoon light was fading, and he was afraid of tripping or falling into a hole.

Buster veered toward the dark line of forest at the edge of the field. And the forest, Charlie knew, marked the top of a ravine that plunged down to the fast-flowing Salmon River. He'd fished there tons of times with Samir. He could hear the roar of the river now, swollen with all the recent rain.

Charlie felt a rising tide of panic. He must not lose control of Buster and have him disappear into the trees.

Buster strained harder on the leash, lunging ahead. He showed no sign of the bad hips Megan had talked about. Bits of straw and spider webs and splats of mud speckled his beautiful chocolate brown coat. Blobs of foamy spit flecked the top of his head.

Charlie gasped for breath.

Buster was moving so fast, it almost seemed— Charlie cringed at how silly the thought was—that he was airborne. But that was impossible. Labradors could run fast, but they couldn't fly.

Charlie tried to shout. He tried to pull back on the leash.

Buster surged ahead with the strength of three dogs.

Something like a sob broke out of Charlie's chest. The dog was out of his control.

Up ahead, Charlie could just make out a row of leaning and rotten fence posts. He tried to dig in his heels. Fence posts meant barbed wire, tangled up with spiky coils of blackberry bramble.

Buster dodged and veered left, definitely back on solid earth ... not that he'd really been flying, Charlie told himself. Then the light dimmed. They were in the trees, a dense thicket of fir and alder. The ground ahead began to fall away, down to the ravine.

Charlie skidded on a moss-covered root and smashed sideways onto his hip. The leash slipped from his fingers. He watched it disappear, like a snake through the grass.

He lay in the dirt, his chest heaving. He could already hear the disappointment in Dr. Anderton's voice: "I'm sorry, Charlie. I said I'd give it a try, but if you can't be responsible, I'm afraid we're going to have to let you go." Megan's uncomprehending face shimmered in his imagination. And what if Buster headed to the road and got hit by a car? What if he met up with a coyote and couldn't hold his own?

And then, unmistakably, hot dog breath rolled over the back of Charlie's neck. He twisted up, and found himself looking into Buster's soft brown eyes.

"You seriously dumb mutt," he muttered. "I'm the one who's supposed to be taking you for a walk, not the other way around."

Buster stepped forward and planted a sloppy hot kiss on Charlie's mouth.

"Not on the lips, you big goof. Yuk."

Charlie stood up and grabbed the leash, wrapping it twice around his hand. He surveyed the damage. His good jeans were slick with mossy slime, and his runners were caked with mud. He was pretty sure his face was streaked with dog drool and dirt. He glanced at his watch. They could still make it back on time.

"Come on, you dufus," he said, picking up the leash.

But Buster didn't budge. Charlie tugged, but the eighty pounds of dog stayed put.

"Now what?" Charlie said.

Chapter 5

RESCUE NUMBER 1

Buster flicked his tail, his gaze steady and serious.

Charlie tugged harder on the leash. "Heel!" he commanded.

Buster danced back and forth, straining toward the river.

"No, boy. We gotta go. Come on, Buster."

It was no use. Charlie's strength was no match for Buster's. The dog began to vocalize in great gulping whines, pointing his nose repeatedly toward the river.

"What is it? What do you see down there?" Charlie squinted into the shadowy gloom at the bottom of the ravine.

Buster barked, a frantic volley of high-pitched yips. He knew something.

Charlie felt the hair on the back of his neck stand up. What was down there? What was making Buster so agitated? "Okay," he said. "I'll go with you. You've got five minutes and then I'm heading back, and you absolutely have to come with me."

The leash snapped taut as Buster plunged down the steep slope. They clambered through the underbrush, leaping fallen branches and dodging muddy dips. Buster stopped short, panting hard, his ears pricked for some message on the air waves.

When he started up again, he kept his head low, his nose inches from the dirt, his tail flicking in a tight, anxious wag.

Charlie checked behind, hoping he'd know how to retrace his steps. It was brighter back up at the edge of the trees, but here the light barely penetrated the canopy of branches overhead. Two minutes more and he'd turn around.

"Poop," he muttered. He'd have to face both Megan and Dr. Anderton. Without Buster. He could see it all now. Dr. Anderton would be saying, "I knew this would never work." And Megan would be looking at him, like it had been a waste of time teaching him anything. And Buster would probably end up getting killed by a pack of coyotes. It could happen. It'd been in the news—lots of coyote attacks in Stanley Park, in Vancouver. And if coyotes were attacking there, in the middle of a big city, it was a definite possibility. No matter what happened, it'd all be Charlie's fault.

He ducked under a low branch, and barely managed to stay upright in the slick mud of the riverbank. This close, the sound of the river was a deafening roar.

Suddenly, the leash went slack. Buster's sides heaved. He turned and looked expectantly at Charlie. Then he pointed his nose toward a dark shape at the river's edge.

"Oh." Charlie sucked in his breath.

Curled up and sound asleep, oblivious to the treacherous currents just inches away, was a very dirty little kid.

Charlie let go of the leash and crept forward. The child was maybe four. His face was covered with muddy streaks. He was wearing red sweatpants and a Superman cape. Charlie edged closer and gently touched the child's shoulder.

He woke with a start and stared, saucer-eyed, at Charlie. "Where's my mom?" he whispered.

Charlie crouched down. "It's okay. We'll find her."

He held out his arms, hesitant, not wanting to scare the kid. But when the boy's lip began to quiver, Charlie gathered him up and struggled to his feet. He adjusted him on his hip and started back up the ravine. The child was heavier than he looked, and Charlie slipped in the ooze and nearly toppled them both. "Where do you think she is?"

The boy wrapped his legs around Charlie's middle. "She's at my house."

"What's your name, anyway?" Charlie asked.

"Jayden." The child stretched to see over Charlie's shoulder. "Big doggie."

Charlie had practically forgotten about Buster. He looked back.

Buster was holding the end of the leash in his mouth and plodding behind them. He raised his head and held Charlie's gaze.

Charlie stared back. How had Buster known? Charlie glanced around at the deep shadow of the riverbed, the roar of the rushing water in his ears. He shook his head and held Jayden closer. Then he turned toward the steep sides of the ravine. He had to find their way back.

It was much lighter when they emerged from the trees at the far end of the field, where Charlie and Buster had set out walking. Charlie tried to set Jayden down to give his arms a rest, but the kid clung like a limpet. Charlie scanned around, searching for a landmark, so he could get his bearings.

In the distance, across the field, he spotted the clinic and, in the same moment, spied the flashing lights of two police cars in the parking lot of the equestrian centre. In the distance, he could just make out people coming toward them. Police. And barking! A tracking dog!

"Jayden, look! Help is coming."

He started to run, Jayden joggling up and down in his arms.

Jayden craned his neck around so he could see, too. "Dog!" he squealed.

Wait till he told Samir. Daring rescue. Child snatched from the jaws of the river. Samir would never believe him. It'd be on the front page of the *Advance*.

A burly officer, led by a sleek black and silver German Shepherd, was the first to reach them. A male and a female officer, with wide grins on their faces, were right on his tail.

Then, running from behind, came another officer, and a woman who had to be Jayden's mom. She had a baby under one arm, and a firm grip on the hand of a little girl, barely bigger than Jayden. The mother looked cold in her short-sleeved T-shirt. Her pink runners were caked with dirt from the trek through the field.

She was gasping for breath by the time she reached them. She gripped the baby with one arm, and bent down to gather Jayden and the girl into a hug, as best she could. She was laughing through her tears.

"Doggie!" Jayden squealed, pointing at the German Shepherd.

Charlie checked behind him. Buster was sitting, still holding the end of the leash in his mouth, the picture of obedience.

The dog handler turned back first, and two of the officers began to lead the reunited family toward the squad cars.

The last officer to arrive pulled out a notepad and turned to Charlie. He held out his hand. "I'm Constable Lee," he said.

Charlie's hand felt small in the officer's grip. "I'm Charlie Campbell. And this is Buster."

Chapter 6

PARTNERS

After Charlie had answered all his questions, Constable Lee slipped his notepad into a pocket. Then he bent down and scratched Buster behind the ears. "Chocolate Labs. My favourite dog. And smart, too." He stood up and gave Buster a last friendly pat. "I never had a dog as a kid."

"Me, neither." Charlie sighed, and took the leash out of Buster's mouth. "But I'm working on it." He watched the policeman stride purposefully back to his car.

Buster shook himself, and a shower of foamy spit flew around his head. He gazed up at Charlie expectantly.

Charlie studied the dog. "Sore hips, eh? Wait till I tell Megan." He gave a slight tug on the leash, and they started off across the field toward the clinic. He kept glancing down at Buster, loping easily at his side. Like his work was done.

The soft sides of Buster's muzzle were hooked up over his teeth, and his tongue hung out to one side. His eyes sought out Charlie's. "Partner," they said.

"Partner," Charlie answered.

The clinic parking lot was empty. Megan had locked up for the night and taped a note on Buster's kennel. "I thought you were taking Buster for a walk, not an expedition. If he starts needing more food, we'll have to take the money out of your paycheque. (Ha, ha, just kidding.) Make sure you lock the kennel. I put your helmet and pack and jacket by your bike. See you Wednesday. Megan."

Charlie held the gate open for Buster, and then took the water pail to the tap at the side of the building. He filled it until the water sloshed against the brim. Then he measured out the kibble, and watched while Buster dove in.

"You're supposed to chew it," Charlie said.

Buster licked out the empty bowl, pushing it around the kennel, so it made a scraping sound on the concrete. Then he sighed, staring over at the kibble bin, as if willing it to open and spill its contents.

Charlie squatted down and rubbed the soft fur on

Buster's chest. It was still warm and damp from exertion.

Buster yawned, a big one that showed the dark brown spots on the pale pink roof of his mouth.

"You knew that little kid was there, didn't you?" Charlie waited, but Buster didn't respond.

Instead, he leaned into Charlie's hand, stretching forward for a quick lick that was practically inside Charlie's nose.

Charlie stood up, pulled the gate closed behind him, and snapped the lock into place. Then he went around to the side to get his bike, and wheeled it back to the kennel.

"Well, goodnight, old fellow." He held the dog's gaze a moment longer, and thought about Dr. Anderton's friends, the couple on Vancouver Island. They might decide to adopt Buster before Wednesday, and he'd never see him again. Or, they might not. Charlie didn't want to think about either possibility.

Buster stood up and wagged his tail. Then he padded over to the mat at the entrance to the doghouse and circled twice, as if looking for the most comfortable spot. He eased himself down, keeping his eyes on Charlie.

Charlie pushed off. It was time to go home.

Chapter 7

NOT YOUR ORDINARY STRAY

Charlie was running late the next morning. The shorts he needed for PE were still in the washing machine, clean but wet. Mom and Dad had decided to have one of their heated "conversations." The toaster had mysteriously stopped working. And he'd barely made it to school on time. He was just about to load his books into his locker, when he heard Samir's voice.

"Finally, you show up." His friend thumped him on the back so hard, his books went flying, and he was pretty sure his neck was dislocated.

"Don't be a jerk," Charlie snarled.

Samir scrambled to pick up the books, while Charlie massaged his neck. "Sorry," he said.

"You don't have to practically kill a guy."

"What're you so mad about? I said I was sorry."

Charlie scowled. It was a cover-up. He was half-afraid he was going to cry.

Samir held out the load of books.

Charlie hitched them under one arm, and leaned against the open door of his locker. "Forget it," he muttered. "Did you study for science?"

"Of course." Samir grinned. "For hours."

"Or maybe five minutes."

Samir frowned. "What's the matter, anyway? You're acting weird."

"*You're* acting weird," Charlie snapped. He did want to tell Samir what was bugging him. But it was hard stuff to talk about. He took a breath. "Next weekend is when my dad goes."

"Oh. I forgot you told me that." Samir squeezed his eyes shut as if he was trying to remember the details. "That's bad."

"Yeah. It's really bad." Charlie studied the timetable he'd taped to the inside of his locker. Math first. He'd only done half the homework questions. What a stupid way to start the day. Then he remembered. "I went to the vet's."

Samir's grin returned. "Did you get to perform surgery?"

"Totally. Quite a few times. It was easy. Well, for me, anyway." Charlie pushed his locker closed and fell into step beside Samir. "But the best part was this stray dog they've got."

Samir hooted. "You're so transparent! You just want the dog, and you're pretending to volunteer so, somehow, you end up getting to keep him."

"I totally want the dog," Charlie agreed. "But let me list for you all the reasons I won't be allowed to have him. Too irresponsible. Don't do my homework. Would probably forget to feed him and he'd die. Had a goldfish, but somehow it died. Mom's allergic. And we might have to move." He stopped shuffling forward with the crowd of kids in the hall, and caused a minor smash-up of bodies. "Oh, and also, Mom bought a new rug and it's white."

"But you saved that robin."

"Doesn't count. Still, you wouldn't believe this dog."

The three-minute warning bell sounded. Charlie had to rush the details about the wild chase and the rescue and the police. "You wouldn't have believed it. He ran straight to the kid, like he was telepathic." Charlie left out the part about Buster running so hard, it looked as if he were flying. As if that could ever happen!

"Don't be dumb. Dogs have better hearing than humans. They hear stuff we can't."

"Like the loud sound of a kid sleeping, at the bottom of a ravine, about a kilometre away."

"No, like the loud sound of a kid crying before he fell asleep." Samir rolled his eyes. "Anyway, he's not psychic. There has to be another explanation."

"Like what?"

"Like, maybe that kid was actually part of the family that originally owned the dog. Maybe the dog was able to pick up the scent, because he remembered it so well. Maybe he knew the kid and that's why—"

"You'd make a terrible detective," Charlie blurted. "Think about it. If it was the lady's dog and he rescued her kid, wouldn't she call out his name, or even just give him a pat or something?"

Samir's face went pink.

"No," Charlie continued. "It was something else. He's not your ordinary stray."

Chapter 8

IT WON'T BE THE SAME

Charlie and Samir didn't talk about Buster anymore that day, but that didn't stop Charlie from thinking about his canine friend all afternoon. Thoughts of Buster still filled his head as he coasted into the driveway.

Dad's car was there. He was never home when Charlie got home from school. It wasn't a good sign.

Charlie dropped his pack on the bench in the hall. "Dad?"

"Up here, son."

Charlie felt like he'd been hit in the gut with a bowling ball. Dad never called him son. Not ever. *Bud*, maybe. *Chuck*, when he wanted to bug him. But never son.

He climbed the stairs. One slow step after another, his legs like lead. He pushed open the door to his parents' bedroom. Dad's suitcase, the one he used when he travelled for business, lay open on the bed. He'd already half-filled two plastic tubs. Dad stood with an armload of shirts, his big frame silhouetted by the light in the closet behind him.

"Hey, Charlie. How was school?"

"Okay." Charlie sat on the edge of the bed and scanned the contents of the tubs. All dad's stuff. A jumble of ties. The hockey jersey he'd won as a door prize. The goofy Christmas sweater with the dancing reindeer.

"Got much homework tonight?" Dad was trying to make it seem like everything was normal.

"Not much. I have to study for a Socials test on Friday, and finish a paragraph for English."

"You want to do something before Mom gets home, maybe kick the soccer ball around?"

"It's okay. I don't feel like playing." Charlie kept his eyes on the carpet, but he felt Dad sit down on the other side of the bed.

"I know."

In the tense quiet of the room, Charlie heard Dad rubbing his fingers through the afternoon stubble on his chin.

Dad cleared his throat. "I'm sorry, Charlie. I know this is hard. It's not something I ever intended to happen, and it doesn't mean I don't—"

"I know," Charlie interrupted. He didn't want to hear it all again. He stood up and took two steps toward the door. Then he stopped and turned. "You already told me. But I still don't get it. What about us?"

"It doesn't mean anything different for you and your brother. Not really. You're still my sons, and I still love you."

"But you won't *be* here."

"Not right here. But I'll still be here in Langley, not very far away. And I still plan to be a big part of everything you do."

Charlie kept his eyes glued to a stain on the carpet, in the shape of a dachshund. He wasn't going to let Dad see him cry. "It won't be the same," he whispered.

Dad rounded the bed in two strides, and pulled Charlie into a hug that squeezed the breath out of him. "You're right. It won't be the same. But I will love you as much as ever, and if you think I'm walking away from your life, you're wrong. Life will go on and you'll grow up, and we'll keep on loving each other. You can trust me on this."

Charlie wriggled free and swiped at his eyes. He was

pretty sure he was having a stroke. His heart felt too big for his ribcage. He sniffed and looked Dad in the eye.

"I think it's probably best if you tell Mom I'm going to need a dog."

Chapter 9

SURGERY

The week sped by. On Friday, Samir spent the whole day trying to talk Charlie into skipping his shift at the vet's. He was still trying when they met at their lockers after last class.

"Come on, Charlie. It's Friday." Samir was practically pleading. "Ryan's got the latest Robo Generation. It's more fun when three play."

"Can't. I've got work."

Samir snorted. "They're not paying you. Say you're sick."

Charlie glanced up at the rain hitting the skylight over the empty hall, and thought about it for a microsecond. By the time he rode to the clinic, he'd be soaked. And Samir's mom would probably make them grilled cheese. But skipping his shift meant he wouldn't see Buster. And what if the couple did come to take Buster, and he didn't even get a chance to say goodbye?

"I can't. It's only my third day, and it'd look bad if I didn't show up." Besides, he thought, Dr. Anderton had been grumpy on Wednesday. Like he wasn't exactly thrilled that Charlie was underfoot. Charlie needed to prove that the vet could rely on him.

He shouldered his locker shut and snapped the lock. "How about Saturday?"

Samir made a face. "Maybe," he grunted.

Once he got outside, Charlie was relieved to find that the rain had subsided into a light drizzle. He fastened his helmet and turned on his flashing taillight. He'd be a little damp when he got to the vet's, but he wouldn't be soaked to the skin.

The first thing he noticed, when he skidded into the parking lot, was that Megan's Corolla wasn't parked in its usual spot. The cowbell over the door clanged as he entered the clinic.

Dr. Anderton called from somewhere in the back. "Is that you, Charlie?"

"Yes, it's me." Charlie hung up his jacket and hurried through the all-purpose space. The door to the surgery room was open, and the extra-bright overhead lights were on.

"Megan's gone home with stomach flu. I could use you in here." Dr. Anderton was already wearing the green scrubs he wore for surgery. He was bent over a German Shepherd, lying on its back in a kind of cradle on the operating table. The anesthetic tube was in its mouth and the dog was out cold. "It's an intestinal blockage," the vet said.

"Sounds serious." Charlie's gut clenched. Maybe he was going to perform surgery. Wait till he told Samir.

The vet's voice was stern. "Wash up." He pointed to the disinfectant soap. "Gloves and gown." He pointed again.

Charlie slipped a surgery apron over his head and pulled on the gloves. His palms were slick with sweat. What did Dr. Anderton want him to do?

"Acute dehydration. Minutes are precious." Dr. Anderton pointed again. "That's the instrument tray."

Charlie looked.

"Under the green linen." The vet sounded tense. "The instruments are arranged in order. Just hand them as I ask for them." He studied Charlie for a moment. "It will smell like blood. Can you handle it?"

In the reception area, the phone rang, and after two rings, the answering machine kicked in.

"Yes." Charlie's knees were shaking so hard, he wondered if they might buckle under him. What did blood even smell like?

Dr. Anderton draped green linen the length of the dog's body, leaving visible only the space where he would make the incision. "Razor," he said.

Charlie was mesmerized by the sight of the dog's flank, moving up and down with his quiet breathing.

"Razor!" The vet's voice was brusque.

Charlie jumped.

It was better than TV. After Dr. Anderton shaved the area bald and flushed it with antiseptic solution, he called for the scalpel. He cut through skin, folding it neatly back and clamping it in place. Then he cut through the next layer of tissue and laid it aside.

The smell hit Charlie. There was hardly any blood to see, but the smell of iron filled his nose. He took two steps backward and leaned against the wall. "Don't faint," he told himself.

Dr. Anderton looked up, his eyebrows knitted tight in an expression of concern.

Charlie pinched his pinkie finger as hard as he could. "I'm okay," he said, and wobbled back to his place.

Dr. Anderton reached into the dog's gut with his gloved hand.

Charlie held his breath.

The vet pulled out a lumpy, segmented tube and laid it on the surgical sheeting. "That's the lower intestine," he said. He moved his fingers along the length of the tube, and, finding nothing, reached in and pulled more from the inside.

"There's the obstruction," he said.

Charlie gasped as he looked at the swollen part of the intestine. It was the size of a Nerf football.

"The smaller scalpel," said the vet. He cut a slit through the side of the intestinal tube and began to pull out a mass of stringy, striped, grey material.

"Shoelaces!" they said together.

The vet laid the partially digested ball of laces to the side and felt along the intestine. "That's all of it," he said. He clamped the tissue together. "Suturing thread and needle."

He pulled the thread in and out until the slit was closed. Then he started the painstaking process of stitching together the layers of tissue and skin. The smell of antiseptic solution filled the room.

"Sterile bandage."

Charlie stared at the tray. There were two bandages on it. He chose the bigger one, and watched, as the vet laid it carefully over the neat line of stitching in the bare patch of skin.

"Get the thermal blanket out of the warmer and tuck it around. Easy, though. No pressure near the incision."

Charlie settled the warm blanket as gently as he could, careful not to disturb the IV line. "How long before he wakes up?"

"He's starting to come to now. He'll be lifting his head in about a quarter of an hour."

Dr. Anderton pulled off his gloves and dropped them into the disposal unit. Charlie did the same.

The vet reached around the dog's chest and shoulders. "You take the hind end. Get a good grip. We'll slide him onto the recovery bed."

The phone in the reception area shrilled again. Charlie tipped his head toward the sound, to indicate that he could get it, but Dr. Anderton shook his head. "Let the machine pick it up," he said. He glanced at the clock on the wall. "Just about time for you to go. Good job today, Charlie. I'm glad you were here."

Charlie helped ease the German Shepherd into a comfortable position inside the recovery kennel, bursting with pride at what Dr. Anderton had said. He couldn't take his eyes off the dog, who was starting to show signs of life. Small shudders. And his eyebrows were twitching. "I still have to walk Buster," he said.

The vet nodded. "I'll finish here and lock up. Then I'll be back later this evening. You're okay to put Buster in for the night?"

"Yeah. I'm good."

"That dog." The vet sighed. "Better not get too attached."

Charlie's heart skipped a beat. He searched Dr. Anderton's face.

"I'm still waiting to hear from the folks on the Island, but I can't keep him much longer. It's not fair to the dog." His expression softened a little. "Still think you want to be a vet?"

Charlie nodded. "More than ever."

"Well, now." Dr. Anderton smiled as he fastened the latch on the kennel. "You'll have to get used to the smell of blood."

Chapter 10

NIGHTMARE

Charlie's heart raced as he grabbed his pack and helmet and slipped out the back door of the clinic. He gulped down a lungful of fresh air. He *would* get used to the smell of blood. But for now, at least, he hadn't fainted, and, on top of that, Dr. Anderton had appreciated his help. And now, the icing on the cake, he got to walk Buster.

The beautiful brown Lab was on his feet, wagging his whole body. He tipped his head back and made a sound, somewhere between a whine and a bark, followed by a series of yips.

Charlie undid the padlock and pushed open the gate, slipping his pack and helmet inside the kennel. He knelt down to clip on the leash, keeping his mouth closed while Buster washed his face with exuberant kisses.

"Oh, yeah. Who's the best dog ever? Right? You're the best dog ever."

Buster flipped onto his back, his legs pawing crazily in the air.

"Itchy?" Charlie scratched the pale pink tummy all over, noticing how the brown fur was speckled with white. Then he picked up the leash. "Okay. That's enough. Let's go."

They started out through the field behind the clinic, as they had done before. The drizzle had stopped, but the clouds were low and black.

Buster trotted at Charlie's side. He was a different dog than the last time. Totally calm, stopping to investigate abandoned sticks, and peeing in a friendly way on anything that smelled interesting.

"Good boy," Charlie said. "This is so much better when you're not acting demented."

Buster doubled the speed of his tail wag, and turned his head back, as if to acknowledge the compliment.

Then he stopped, ears pricked.

Charlie listened. All he could hear was the distant hum of traffic on Saddlehorn. He glanced back at the clinic. It looked a little forlorn on this dull, grey, late afternoon. He couldn't see any sign of lights. Dr. Anderton must have already locked up and headed home for his supper. Charlie shivered. A mist had begun to form in low pockets in the field around him, as the colder air of approaching night met the warmer earth.

Without warning, the leash snapped tight, pulling painfully where he'd double wrapped it around his wrist.

Charlie braced himself. Not again!

Buster broke into a run.

Charlie caught himself before he fell, and started to sprint.

This time, Buster veered east, away from the forest, toward the sprawling equestrian centre that neighboured the vet clinic.

"Heel!" Charlie yelled. "Heel!"

But it was no use. Buster pounded ahead like a dog possessed.

Charlie hung on, eyes on the ground in front of him, his breath coming in ragged gasps. The leash dug into his wrist.

Then he saw it. A barbed-wire fence. Three strands of barbs looming closer by the second. He tried to remember what he knew about a dog's eyesight. He had a sinking feeling it was one of their less developed senses.

In a frantic bid to avoid being cut to shreds, Charlie put on a burst of speed. When he was almost alongside Buster, he lunged. He grabbed the dog around his back and chest, and closed his eyes for the crash.

But there was no crash. Instead, the dog's gait smoothed into a gentle and controlled lope. Charlie lifted his eyes from Buster's flank and saw, below him, the black and deadly line of the barbed wire fence, slashed across the darkened field where they had been running. As they rose higher, the clinic receded into the distance, and the cars on Saddlehorn became small specks of light.

Charlie clung to the dog's body with his arms and legs, and buried his face in the warm fur of Buster's back.

He was not flying. He could not be flying. Dogs did not fly, except in books and dreams. This was a nightmare like he'd never experienced. Wait till he told Samir about this one.

Chapter 11

FLIGHT

Charlie closed his eyes and shook his head. But when he opened them again, he was still in the nightmare.

A sharp pain screamed in his wrist. The leash dug in so tight, it was cutting off the circulation. He eased his grip on Buster to try to loosen it. But the moment he did, he slipped sideways.

Panicking, he grabbed at Buster's back and dragged himself upright. His heart pounded at the thought of falling from this height.

When his breathing finally slowed, he forced himself to look down. And down and down. It was not a nightmare. They *were* flying. Not as high as the clouds. But as high as the treetops. Wind like ice sliced across the exposed skin of his back, where his jacket was riding up. He laid his cheek on the fur of Buster's back, choking back his terror. Just breathe, he told himself.

He mustered his courage and lifted his head again. Gently, gently, he shimmied forward, trying to see Buster's face.

The dog turned his head toward Charlie.

Even in the almost darkness, Charlie could see the expression on Buster's face, determined and serious. "Trust me," it said.

Charlie tightened his grip. "Oh, Buster," he whispered. "I hope I don't throw up like I did on the plane that time."

Buster faced forward again, his velvety ears blowing back in the wind, his paws churning steadily through the empty air.

Charlie looked down, trying to get his bearings. They had veered south, past Charlie's own neighbourhood. He tried to spot his house, but there was too little light now, and the fog had started to drift in here as well.

Up ahead, the headlights on Fraser Highway twinkled in a moving stream. But once they'd crossed the highway, Buster veered east again, keeping to the dark patches of forest and open fields. No one would see them in the semi-darkness.

Soon they were directly above the nearby community

of Aldergrove, and starting to bank and turn in a gentle curve to the right. There was the elementary school, and behind it, the soccer field, where Charlie had played in a tournament last fall.

Buster banked more steeply.

Charlie pitched forward as they began a sharp descent. He cringed at the thought of the hard-packed gravel surface below, and braced for impact. He squeezed his eyes shut.

Beneath him, the rhythm of the dog's body slowed and slowed. Charlie opened one eye.

Buster touched down as light as a cat.

Charlie rolled forward over the dog's head, and landed in a sprawling heap. He lay still, gulping in air.

Buster stood over him, licking his face. But there was no time for talk. The dog shook himself and started to trot toward the portables at the back of the school.

The leash snapped tight.

Charlie scrambled to his feet and checked over his shoulder. He caught a whiff of garbage, and could just make out the big industrial garbage bins behind the portable classrooms. It was the loneliest part of the schoolgrounds. If he cried out, no one would hear him.

It was exactly the kind of place he didn't want to be in alone. In the dark.

Chapter 12

RESCUE NUMBER 2

In the shadowy, deserted space behind the portables, Charlie could barely see where to put his feet. He trained his eyes on Buster's inky silhouette, and tried not to think about who or what might be hiding ahead of him in the darkness.

At the corner of the nearest portable, Buster hesitated, one front paw suspended mid-step. He cocked his head.

Charlie listened as he unwound the leash from his wrist and let it drop.

Voices.

Buster stepped forward, into the pool of yellow light from a dim security lamp over the portable door.

Charlie followed, inches behind Buster.

It was like a scene from a movie. A kid was on the ground in the play area, his face in the dirt. He was surrounded by three guys in black hoodies, all of them bigger than Charlie. One of them had his foot on the kid's back, pinning him down, while the other two jeered. All of them looked up, open-mouthed.

Charlie fought the urge to run.

The kid on the ground turned his head, his eyes wide with terror. A trickle of blood oozed from his nose.

The one with his foot on the kid's back shifted his weight, and scuffed a spray of fine gravel into the kid's face.

Buster moved forward two steps. All eyes turned to the dog.

Charlie swallowed. The gang of bullies didn't know much about dogs, if they thought a Labrador was any kind of attack dog.

He had to make a decision. Should he run or act?

He cleared his throat. "You should let him go. He's just a kid." His voice sounded tiny. He'd thought he might tell them to pick on someone their own size, but the other two stepped in on either side of their leader, and his mouth clamped shut.

Beside him, Buster tensed, his tail strangely still.

Charlie gathered his courage again. "If you don't let him go, I'll call the police."

The group erupted into screams of laughter.

"Oh, tough guy," the leader mocked. "Maybe I have to borrow your cell phone." He started to amble toward Charlie.

A low, menacing growl burbled in Buster's throat.

The three shrank back. Charlie could tell they were trying to measure the fierceness of the dog.

"It's just a Lab," one of them said. He sounded like he was trying to convince himself the dog didn't pose a threat.

Buster growled again. His teeth glinted where his lips curled up.

One of the gang stepped forward and raised his hand, as if to strike the dog.

Buster sprang. He caught the boy's upraised hand in his jaws and, with the force of his weight, landed like something spring-loaded on the boy's chest, knocking him flat.

Buster's body was rigid with fury. He pinned the boy to the gravel, his jaws still closed on the hand.

The other two approached warily, as if to save their friend.

Buster's tail twitched, his eyes fixed on them. He crouched and sprang again, flying right over his first victim. He dropped down and lunged at one of the others, snapping and snarling, and tearing at the fellow's jacket. The roar from Buster's throat was chilling.

The boy who had been knocked down first struggled to his feet and fled with the leader. Buster ripped one last jaw-full of fabric out of his second victim's jacket, and then pulled back to watch him struggle to his feet and disappear, running into the darkness.

Charlie stood frozen in place, testing the silence for any sign the three bullies were coming back. But there was only the din of traffic on Fraser Highway, and, after a moment or two, the sound of deep quiet sobs from the kid, still curled up on the gravel.

Chapter 13

HOME SAFE

Buster trotted back to Charlie and licked his hand. Then he sat down, his sides still heaving.

Charlie exhaled the breath he'd been holding. He knelt down beside the boy on the ground, and put his hand tentatively on the kid's back. He could see where his jacket was ripped and wet with sweat. "It's okay," Charlie said. "They're gone. Come on, I'll help you up."

The sobs continued, long and gut-wrenching.

"Come on," Charlie urged. "We should get out of here. You can do it. Unless ... are you badly hurt?"

The boy pulled himself into a sitting position and wiped his eyes. The blood from his nose had dried in a broad streak across his cheek. His hair, metallic pink in the dim light, was plastered in damp strands against his face.

"You okay?" Charlie asked. He hunched down more,

trying to get eye contact with the boy. "What's your name, anyway?"

"Tyler."

"What happened? Who were those guys?"

"I don't know. Losers."

"Losers and bullies," Charlie agreed. "They pick on someone smaller to make themselves feel bigger. Real tough." He touched the side of the boy's face. "There's a bit of blood here."

Tyler rubbed his cheek with his sleeve.

Buster heaved a sighing grunt and pushed himself to standing. He looked up at Charlie, and then started to lick the blood from Tyler's face.

Charlie followed the dog's progress. "I wonder why they jumped you, anyway. What were you doing back here?"

"Short cut," the boy said, and spat some dirt out of his mouth. He rubbed the back of his neck. "Probably because of my hair." He locked eyes with Charlie. "Some guys have a problem with pink."

Charlie shook his head in disgust. He stood up and reached a hand down to Tyler. "Come on, let's get out of here." He picked up the end of Buster's leash. "I guess we'd better go to the police."

Tyler shook so hard, his teeth chattered. "No way." He gulped in a few mouthfuls of air. "I go to the police and I'm dead."

"But you've got to. Somebody has to get those guys, or they'll just keep on."

"Not me. I'm not taking any chances. I'll just keep my mouth shut and stay out of their way."

"But—"

"Forget it." He peered into the shadows around them. "Thanks, and everything. But I'm just getting out of here."

Tyler brushed off the seat of his pants and headed toward the street. After a moment's hesitation, Charlie followed, with Buster in tow.

"Where are you going?"

"Home."

"I'll walk with you if you want. Is it far?"

Tyler looked straight into Charlie's face. His eyes glittered with tears. "That'd be great. It's not far, really."

They walked in silence, Buster plodding at Charlie's side, back out into the lights and steady traffic in front of the school. Tyler pointed ahead and to the left. "I live a block further along here, and then another block down that way."

Charlie nodded. He wondered what time it was.

"How did you happen to be there?" Tyler asked finally. "It's like you dropped out of nowhere, just in time to save me."

Charlie choked. "Dunno. Just happened to be in the right place at the right time. And anyway, it's not like I saved your life or anything."

"I don't know." Tyler appeared to think this over. "I guess if it had got really bad, you could have called the police."

Charlie snorted. "With my imaginary cell phone. Might have been quicker to shoot them with my imaginary gun."

Tyler stopped and stared. "You threatened to call the police with a phone you didn't have? Nice."

They had reached a townhouse complex. The low-rent kind, with cars everywhere, and toys in the yards, and abandoned junk heaped up in carports. Charlie smelled onions cooking.

"This is my place." Tyler pointed at Number 12. The blinds were down, no light peeking through.

Charlie reached into his pocket for his mini Maglite and scanned the dark entranceway. "Doesn't look like anybody's home. Do you have a key?"

"Yeah." Tyler considered the empty townhouse. "There's never anybody here when I get home. My mom won't get in till around nine." He sounded resigned.

"You're sure you're okay? We could still call the police."

"Forget it. I'm okay."

There was an awkward silence for a minute.

Tyler leaned down and ran his hand over Buster's warm back. "You don't actually look like an attack dog, but you sure turned it on for those guys."

Buster retreated behind Charlie and peed on a power pole.

"Well, I guess I'll see you. Thanks a lot."

Charlie wanted to hold onto the moment. Do something for Tyler. Try to make it better. He pointed to Tyler's hair. "I think it looks good, actually."

Tyler's mouth erupted in a grin. He ran his fingers through his hair, still damp and clinging to his face. Then he gave a quick wave and headed up his walk.

Charlie watched as the younger boy let himself in. A light appeared inside, and Charlie heard the click of the lock.

Chapter 14

CAMPFIRE

Charlie looked up and down the street. It was crowded with parked cars. Dads and moms and kids, home for their suppers. The smell of macaroni and onions in the air. From inside the nearest townhouse, a whistle shrilled. Hockey on the TV. Dinners on laps. Whole families together.

A lump formed in Charlie's throat. He leaned down and scratched Buster under the chin.

Buster flopped down and began to chew his hind paw.

Charlie knelt beside him. "Now what?" he said. "What's the plan? We need to get home."

Buster left his paw dangling in mid-air and tipped his head to one side.

"I'm not walking."

Buster sighed and shimmied to his feet. He licked Charlie's hand and started to walk, his toenails clicking softly on the deserted sidewalk.

"I mean it," Charlie said, falling into step. "It would take an hour to walk back." He glanced at his watch. "Mom's going to kill me, as it is."

They turned off Tyler's street and onto the busier one. Cars whizzed by. A horn honked. Traffic lights ahead blinked green.

A movement up ahead, just past the school, stopped Charlie dead in his tracks. He pulled up sharply on Buster's leash. It was the same guys who'd jumped Tyler. They were hunched around a bike, on its side in the grass, in front of an apartment building. Their backs were to him. He spotted the red glow of a cigarette. Even in the dim illumination from the streetlights, he knew for certain who it was.

Charlie fought the urge to run. Instead, he inched backward to the power pole he'd just passed and slipped behind it, pulling Buster in close.

His heart raced. What to do?

Buster sat on his haunches, eyebrows furrowed, looking up at Charlie.

And then, reflected in the gleam from Buster's eyes, Charlie became aware of flashing lights.

Across the street, a police car had pulled up behind a shiny black pickup truck. The officer inside appeared to be looking down at a screen. Running the licence plate number, probably.

Charlie glanced back down at Buster. What were the odds of a police car showing up, right when you needed it?

He peered out from behind the power pole. "No way," he muttered, disgusted by what he saw. The three guys were still there, but one of them had started to stomp on the bike with both feet. The sickening, pinging sound of spokes snapping stretched all the way back to Charlie.

The jerk-faces. First Tyler and now somebody's bike. It wasn't fair. There was no way he was taking a chance on confronting them again, but there was something he *could* do. He cinched up the leash, looked left and right, and dashed across the street. He slipped around to the far side of the police car, feverishly hoping his sudden movement hadn't attracted attention from the gang.

He knocked on the window.

The officer looked up, startled. She flipped a switch and the window slid down. "Yeah?" she said.

Charlie started to talk in a whisper.

"Sorry, what?" she said, pushing the computer away. "Say again?"

Charlie spoke a little louder. "See those guys?" He pointed, and the officer cranked her head around.

"Yeah?" she said.

"I just saw them beat up a little kid. I was too scared to do anything." Charlie's gut twisted as the fib slid easily out of his mouth.

"Where'd this happen?" she barked.

Charlie could tell she wanted to get on with running the licence plate and writing up the ticket.

"Out behind the school. Between the portables and the school." Charlie ransacked his brain for a way to try to get her to do something. "I was hiding, but I saw them do it. They practically killed him. And now they're destroying someone's bike."

"Oh, geez," she said. "All right." She got out of the car and marched up to the driver's door of the pickup. "It's your lucky day," she said to the driver. "Ten kilometres over the speed limit. Think about it." She smacked the roof of the car and turned back to Charlie. "So, where's the kid?"

"I don't know," Charlie said. It was the least he could do. Tyler had been pretty clear, he didn't want to have anything to do with the police. "I just know he was able to get up and walk away, once they were done with him."

"And what's your name, then?"

"It's Charlie. But I have to go. I'm really late, and my mom's going to go ballistic if I don't show up, like in the next minute.

She studied Charlie. Then her steely gaze turned to the three guys.

Charlie could tell she was wrestling with making a decision.

She glanced heavenward, shook her head, and slammed back into the car.

Charlie watched as she shoulder-checked and did a U-turn, right in the middle of the street. She'd turned her flashing light off. *Yes*, he thought. Surprise attack.

He wanted desperately to know what happened next, but he knew an opportunity when he saw one. It was time to get out of here. He tightened his hold on the leash, waited till there was a break in the traffic, and sprinted back across the street.

Then it was Buster's turn.

Charlie let the leash go slack, so the dog could take the lead.

Buster started slowly. Then he picked up the pace, his head up, ears alert. As soon as they reached the edge of the schoolyard, Buster veered off the sidewalk toward the school.

Charlie dragged his feet. "I'm not going in there," he whispered. He scanned the empty space. There was nobody. Just dark corners and places to hide. Behind the school, the portables loomed.

Buster strained forward.

"This is stupid, Buster." Charlie's voice quavered. His heart thrashed as the leash snugged tighter on his wrist.

Buster moved ahead like an arrow, straight for the back of the school.

Charlie chewed on his lower lip as Buster dragged him forward.

There was the play area where Tyler had been pinned.

There were the portables.

And behind them, the playing field, unlit and lonely.

Then it came to him. It made sense. Here was a dark spot with no one around. Enough room to take off and no one to see. Charlie's heart hammered at the thought of the flight ahead.

In the shadow behind the first portable, Buster sat and shoved his cold nose into Charlie's hand.

"So, how do we do this?" Charlie wondered aloud. He moved behind the dog and bent down and wrapped his arms around Buster's chest.

Buster began to surge forward, in a powerful run.

Charlie scrambled to get his feet under him, wincing as the gravel tore at his knees.

They were airborne in seconds. Charlie pulled his legs up, easing them carefully around the dog's girth, so as not to interfere with his stride.

He clung on, feeling the steady, rhythmic churning beneath him, and the icy touch of the air streaming past. He studied the ground below. The red taillights of cars on the Fraser Highway streamed off to the east and west. Soon, the lights of Aldergrove had receded into the distance. To the north, an eerie white light reflected off snow-capped peaks. Charlie searched desperately for a glimpse of the clinic.

Just as he was sure he had spotted it, Buster's nose thrust out to his left, and, for a moment, he seemed to tread air, off balance. Empty space yawned below them, and Charlie screamed in terror.

Buster banked further left, until he was heading due south.

Charlie buried his face in the dense fur of the dog's shoulder ruff. "No, Buster," he pleaded. "I've got homework. No more rescue missions."

But Buster churned ahead, faster than ever.

Charlie raised his head and peered over the dog's shoulder. The Fraser Highway disappeared behind them. Far to his left, Charlie could see the trucks on 264th Street slowing down, as they approached the border crossing between Canada and the United States.

Buster shifted direction again. Now he was headed west, so they were paralleling the invisible line between the two countries.

"Don't cross over it, Buster." Charlie's voice was sharp with panic. "Don't even think about it. I don't want to be the object of an international incident."

The idea percolated in Charlie's brain. "I mean it, Buster. We could get shot down!"

Charlie slid forward, so he was leaning hard on Buster's shoulders. They were descending. Below them,

Zero Avenue stretched east and west. He'd driven it lots of times with his family, when they'd gone down to do some cross-border shopping. Shopping! Would he ever get to do it again? With Mom and Dad. In a car. In a world that was normal.

As they dropped, the miles of dark empty forest along the border began to materialize. Now they were just above the treetops, and the Christmassy smell of evergreen forest reached up and enveloped them. Charlie looked down. Maybe he could jump, escape from this nightmare flight. But even at this height, it would mean certain death.

Buster banked again. And there was another smell—smoke.

They circled and the smell was stronger. Charlie craned his neck to try to catch a glimpse of fire in the dark forest.

Then he spotted it. A flicker of orange. A tiny campfire. Barely large enough for the light from the flames to penetrate the wall of trees, and not enough smoke to be detected, until they were almost directly overhead.

Charlie laid his head on Buster's back. He couldn't think about what was coming next.

And then, as abruptly as Buster had changed direction before, they were ascending again, away from the mysterious campfire. Icicles of wind pricked Charlie's face as they picked up speed. In the distance, once again, snow-capped mountains shimmered.

He could have whooped for joy. North. They were going back. Carefully, he reached a hand up to scratch behind Buster's ear. Below him, Buster's sides heaved with the effort of flying.

Buster turned his head a little. Beads of condensation glistened on the side of his velvet muzzle, and Charlie wondered what light they were reflecting.

It was only a matter of minutes before Charlie picked out Saddlehorn Hill and the veterinary clinic beyond.

The building was almost completely dark, except for the security light over the back door. In the shadows, Charlie could just make out one familiar car parked out back by Buster's kennel.

Chapter 15

DINNER FOR THREE

Charlie braced himself for the landing, but Buster touched down with the grace of a dragonfly. Charlie slid smoothly over Buster's head, coming to rest on his stomach on the rough grass.

Buster's hot breath was on his neck. Charlie lifted his head and scanned the dark corner of the field where they'd landed. He clenched the leash tighter, struggled to his feet, and sprinted toward the clinic. Mom would be frantic.

"Mom!" he called as he emerged from the shadows. The front wheel of his bike was sticking out of the trunk of the car. At least he wouldn't have to ride home in the dark.

She was pacing back and forth behind her car, looking like she was ready to strangle him. She turned sharply. "Charlie! It's almost seven o'clock. Where've you been. I've been worried sick."

"I know. I'm sorry." The flying would have to be a secret. You didn't just tell your parents a thing like that. "I—we got a little carried away on our walk. And then—" The lie floated out of his mouth. "Buster got his collar caught in barbed wire, and it took me forever to get him loose."

Buster leaned on Charlie's leg and licked his hand. It's true, he seemed to say.

Mom looked down at Buster, as if seeing him for the first time. Her face softened. She let out a deep sigh. "In ten minutes, I was going to call the police. That's how upset I was. You need to let me know what's going on."

"Yes, Mom," Charlie said. It was the perfect opportunity to bring up the cell phone question, but he had to prioritize. Dog first. Phone later. Not too much at once.

Mom reached forward and gave Buster a quick pat on the head. "What about him?"

"He goes in here." Charlie opened the kennel and checked the water bowl.

Buster shuffled toward the gate, his sad eyes on Mom.

"Look at him coax." Mom shook her head. "Not a chance, old fella."

Charlie filled the kibble bowl, and stood back to watch Buster dig in.

Buster hoovered the contents, barely chewing, and licked the bowl clean. Then he stared at the kibble bin.

"That's all you get, big fellow. Megan's orders."

Buster's head drooped. He gave them each one last look. Then, shoulders sagging and tail limp, he disappeared into the doghouse in the corner of the enclosure.

Charlie locked the gate.

"He seems like a good old dog," Mom said as she slid into the driver's seat. "It's a pity someone doesn't adopt him."

Charlie knew an opening when he saw one.

"He's the best, Mom. House trained. Loves people. Too old to eat much."

Her voice was firm. "We're not getting a dog. We've been through this. Especially not now."

Right. Dad.

"And besides," she added, "you couldn't even remember to feed the fish you had. I just know who'd end up looking after a dog."

"Mo-om. It was a hand-me-down guppy. I didn't

even want a guppy." Charlie crossed his arms over his chest. "And besides, I was eight."

"Well, don't get any ideas, anyway." She accelerated onto Saddlehorn. The conversation was closed. For now.

Charlie stared out the side window into darkness. There was no question in his mind. Buster was meant to be his dog. Buster was his destiny. They were a team. He sucked in a deep gulp of air and gripped the armrest, as he relived the steep descent over the mysterious campfire.

"It's pretty dark out there, where you walk Buster." Mom's voice broke into his thoughts. "Do you think it's safe?"

Charlie held back a grin. "The field is safe, Mom. That should be the least of your worries."

"What's that supposed to mean?"

"It just means it's safe—safer than walking along Saddlehorn, where there's no sidewalk." Charlie pressed his lips together. Now, as for the flying, and the gangs, and the international border, and the strange campfire in the night, that was a different story. That was probably not safe.

His thoughts went back to Buster. Two rescue missions already. He shivered, and a picture of Tyler's dark townhouse rose up in his mind. Tyler's mom had not been there to pick him up when he was in trouble. What would have happened to Tyler, if he and Buster had not shown up when they did?

And what about Buster? Another night stuck away in a dark and lonely kennel. And another day closer to when the couple from the Island might decide he was their dog. Or not. Charlie glanced across at Mom as she turned up their driveway. Now was not the time to let up. Seconds counted. He wheeled his bike into the garage, deep in thought. He needed a strategy.

Inside the house, the lights were on, and Charlie could smell dinner. Mark was in the kitchen, stirring something on the stove and talking on his phone. He made a face at Charlie and mouthed the word, "Stew."

But something felt different, and Charlie knew his world had changed. He dropped his backpack by the door and listened. Upstairs, all was quiet.

Mom paused, before hanging her jacket on its hook by the door. "He's not here. He moved into the apartment this morning."

She looked sad, as if she was about to apologize. "Charlie, I know this is—"

Charlie thought about Tyler, alone in the dark townhouse. His mom wouldn't even be home yet. "I know," he said. "It's okay." He forced his mouth into a smile. "So, what's the hold-up? Let's eat."

Mom looked confused, like she'd been expecting something different. She leaned against the door frame, studying him. "Good idea," she said. "Let's eat."

When Mark finally set his phone down, Mom put a steaming bowl at each place. It was the same table where they always sat, only tonight, it was set for three. Charlie pulled his chair in closer to the table. Mom and Mark did the same thing.

The soft light from above shone in a warm glow around them. Nobody said a word, but it was as if a loop that circled them had been tightened a notch.

Mom broke the silence.

"All right," she said. "Tell me about your day."

Chapter 16

THE SIGHTING

Friday morning of the following week, Charlie had already stuck his helmet on his head when he saw the flat. He raced back into the house, hoping Mark was still there. He had a math test first period, so he couldn't be late, and Mom had already left for work. Luckily, Mark was still in the bathroom off the kitchen, the powder room as Mom called it, gelling his hair.

"Can I get a ride with you and Nick? My tire's flat." Even though Charlie had moved up to the secondary school in September, Mark hadn't hung around him much, but maybe today would be an exception.

"I guess. Nick'll be here in a sec." A horn blared in the driveway. "No. Nick's here now." Mark pushed his hair up at the side with the last of the gel on his fingers, and then shouldered his backpack. Charlie followed him to the front door and locked it behind them.

Nick's ancient Mazda was belching clouds of black smoke into the neighbourhood. Charlie piled into the back seat, coughing.

"Hey, Charlie." Nick grinned, as he backed up and turned into the street. "Not biking today?"

"Flat tire."

"Too bad. Hey, I saw you in Aldergrove last week, walking some dog. Got a girlfriend out there?"

Charlie could feel his face turning beet red. "In Aldergrove?" He made his voice sound sarcastic. Everyone knew Aldergrove was the competition. "Why would anyone go to Aldergrove?"

"I'm sure it was you, walking along by the school?"

Mark turned around and looked at his brother with interest.

"Couldn't have been. I was working," Charlie said, trying to take control.

"You?" Nick sounded doubtful. "When did you get a job?"

"It's not a real job. I volunteer at the vet's. He doesn't pay me, but I go three days a week, just like a real job."

Nick narrowed his eyes at him through the rear-view mirror. "You work for nothing?"

"Uh-huh." Nick made it sound like the world's stupidest idea, but at least they'd moved on from the Aldergrove sighting.

"Dumb," Nick said.

Charlie thought about telling him how cool it was. But he knew Nick wouldn't get it. Nick worked two part-time jobs, and the money was the whole point.

"Anyway, it was last Friday I saw you."

"Couldn't have been. Must have been my twin." *Come on Nick, let it go*, Charlie thought. He watched Mark pull down the vizor mirror and poke at the sides of his hair some more. He thought about telling him about the blob of gel on his ear, but decided it was too small to really matter.

"Well, it was totally you. And it was a Lab, or a dog like that."

Charlie's heart raced. "Okay, Nick. It was me. There's this dog at the vet's that can fly, and we took a little trip to Aldergrove. Just a test flight. Then next week, we're flying to Disneyland. He's super fast. For a dog. And next week, we're also taking the flying cats."

Nick glared at him in the rear-view mirror and hit the volume button on the radio.

Charlie sucked in a deep breath, and resisted the urge to plug his ears. He hated rap.

Mark shifted around in his seat. "How you going to get to the vet's today if your bike's broken?" he asked.

Charlie couldn't stop looking at the blob of gel. Maybe he should mention it, after all. "I don't know yet. I have to think of something."

Nick waited for the crossing guard in front of the school to return to the sidewalk with her sign. Then he roared into the student parking and squeezed the car into a spot, narrowly missing the dusty SUV on the passenger side.

"I'll take you. I know where the vet is. It's on my way to work." He reached into the back seat for a stack of books. "Meet me here at three."

"Great. I'll be here," Charlie said. "And thank you." But his brother and Nick were already out of earshot and headed toward the gym. Charlie shouldered his backpack, and joined the crowd of kids streaming up to the main entrance.

Samir caught up with him, just as he was about to go through the big double doors. "Hey, Charlie. Where've you been?"

"Hi." Charlie stopped short, puzzled. "Nowhere. What do you mean?"

"It was open gym after school. Everyone stayed."

"There was open gym yesterday?"

"Duh. Like there is every Thursday."

Charlie wracked his brain. Where *had* he been. Samir was his best friend. He always went to open gym with him. Then he remembered. He'd gone straight home, hoping Dad would stop by for more boxes. But he hadn't. "I don't know. I guess I had homework."

Samir's eyebrows shot up. "You okay?"

"Yeah, great. I guess I'm just super busy, trying to keep up with school and the job at the vet's." Super. That was the right word. He had a Super Dog, and he was Super Rescuer. He'd been flying. Oh, God, he'd been flying. Charlie managed a weak smile.

"Anyway, if you're not too busy studying—" Samir's voice dripped with sarcasm. "Mom says it's okay for you to sleep over tonight."

It was the last thing he wanted to do. Too much going on. But Samir was going to think he didn't want to hang out. "I'll ask, but I'm sure I can. I have to work, so I'll come over after dinner."

"Well, phone me when you know." Samir sped off into the crowded hall.

Charlie hit the stairs and headed for his math test. All around him, kids scurried to class. They looked so chill, like their dads weren't leaving, and they didn't have a care in the world. And not one of them, Charlie thought, was thinking about flying.

Wingless.

On a dog.

Chapter 17

POPULATION CONTROL

Except for his math test, where he'd actually had to concentrate, Charlie spent the whole day unable to think about anything but Buster. In Socials, his teacher made a comment about him being lost in space, and in PE, he took a volleyball to the head because he wasn't paying attention. He couldn't. He was miles away in his thoughts. Clinging to Buster. The wind icy against his face.

By the time he met Nick at his car after school, the weather had turned cold, and it had started to drizzle. He made himself talk nonstop the whole way to the vet's. He did not want to give Nick a chance to revisit the "Aldergrove Incident."

Nick squealed to a stop in front of the clinic. Charlie got out and watched him peel off, in the usual cloud of black smoke. He pulled open the clinic door, barely conscious of the now familiar clang of the cow bell.

Megan was spray-dusting the display case in the reception area. The case was full of veterinary oddities pickled in glass jars, the latest addition being the ball of laces extracted from the German Shepherd's intestine. Dr. Anderton was just saying goodbye to a lady holding a dachshund, with a rhinestone choker around its neck.

Megan glanced up. "Charlie! You'd better roll up your sleeves. We've got an SPCA neutering clinic happening in about ten minutes. You're going to be busy."

"Cool. What can I do?" Charlie's heart pounded. Every day, he was asked to do something new. It was always a little nerve-wracking, until he figured things out. What if he blew it? What if he didn't do it right?

"I think you'll be doing something of a highly technical nature." Her voice was low and serious.

"Like what?" He knew Megan too well. He was suspicious.

"Like carrying kennel cages in from the SPCA truck, and then ... guess what?"

"Let me guess ... maybe carrying them back out when they're done?"

"The boy's a genius. And he works for free," Megan hooted.

"Right." Charlie snorted and hung up his jacket.

"Seriously, Charlie." Megan looked repentant. "Probably some other stuff, too."

"I can hardly wait," he said as sarcastically as he could. Then he headed into the kennel area to check out the inmates. A boxer pup with a serious underbite pounded the cage front with his paws, trying to get Charlie's attention. A bunny with a bandaged ear blinked her pink eyes in his direction. The rest of the cages were empty.

But it was Buster Charlie really wanted to see. He hurried out of the kennel area, down the hall, past the coat hooks, and out the back door.

Buster was on his feet, wagging his whole body. Then he plunged his face into his water bowl and lapped furiously, as if he'd only just remembered he was thirsty.

Charlie was about to unlock the kennel door for a quick pet, when the SPCA truck rumbled into the parking area. The driver hopped out, wrenched up the big sliding door, and lowered a ramp into place with a loud clang. Charlie whistled—six crates. He propped the clinic door open and approached.

"Hi," he said. "I'm Charlie. I'm volunteering here. Need some help?"

The driver looked up in surprise, and Charlie had a chance to admire the tattooed image of a heron that stretched up her neck toward her ear. "You got it." She laughed and held up the first cage. "I'm Kim, by the way. I'm a volunteer, too."

They worked together, and soon had all the crates lined up on a counter in the all-purpose room. Megan surveyed the lot. "All puppies," she said. "Charlie, here's a job for you. I need the weight of each one." She pointed to the small animal scale. "And you record the weight here on the chart attached to each crate."

Charlie couldn't keep the smile from his face. Megan trusted him. She'd given him a real job.

Megan disappeared into the surgery room. Kim gave Charlie an enthusiastic thumbs up. "I'll be in the waiting room if anybody needs me."

By the time he'd recorded the weights of all six puppies, Dr. Anderton and Megan had put on scrubs and swung into action. The bright lights lit up every corner of the surgery room, and the sharp smell of sterilizing solution filled the air.

Charlie watched through the window in the door, as Megan lifted the first little brown ball of fur up to the platform. She held the dog gently but firmly, while Dr. Anderton shaved a patch of skin on its foreleg, where he would inject the anaesthetic that would put the pup into a sound sleep.

Charlie sighed. He wanted to be right there, so he could watch every step up close, like he had with the German Shepherd. But he had an important job to do, tucking sterile towelling into each little kennel in preparation for the return of a groggy and disoriented pup. Dr. Anderton even insisted on a tiny hot water bottle underneath the towelling. One more way to reduce the dog's discomfort after the surgery.

The clinic was quiet, except for the muffled sound of voices coming from the surgery room. The answering machine was handling calls. Exhausted by his fierce efforts to be noticed, the boxer with the underbite had flaked out in a corner of his kennel.

Dr. Anderton worked quickly. Charlie observed through the window as well as he could, while he waited for the first pup to be done.

As soon as he saw Megan lift the limp bundle, he pushed open the door with his foot and reached out for the dog. He carefully slipped on the puppy-sized lampshade collar and snapped it closed. Then he tucked the pup into the waiting kennel, pulling the towelling around to make it as cozy and warm as possible.

By the time the SPCA truck rolled out with its sleepy cargo, it was almost 5:30. Charlie's heart raced. It was time for Buster.

Chapter 18

DUE SOUTH

Buster was on his feet, his face jammed against the chain link, his tail making frantic revolutions.

Charlie opened the padlock and knelt down to clip on the leash. "Sit," he said firmly.

Buster sat, his tail swishing over the gravel.

"Buster," Charlie began.

Buster maintained eye contact.

"This is a walk. Not," Charlie glanced around, "not a fly."

Buster stood up, front paws bouncing.

"Sit," Charlie repeated. "I mean it. I'm going to a sleepover. I have to get home. So. Let's be clear. This is a W-A-L-K walk."

Buster's gaze shifted so he was looking vaguely into the distance.

Not good, Charlie thought.

Buster led off across the parking lot, stopping to pee on a tinfoil burger wrapper. Then he shook himself and headed for the vacant field behind the clinic.

It had started to drizzle again. Charlie stopped to zip up his jacket.

Buster stopped, too. He lifted a front paw, his nose to the wind.

Charlie double-wrapped the leash around his wrist. "No, Buster," he warned. "Remember the sleepover."

Buster turned to look at Charlie, suddenly panting, his tongue lolling out. "I'm sorry," his eyes said.

He broke into a full gallop. Charlie sprinted, knowing with absolute certainty what was coming. A voice in his head screeched, "Let go of the leash! Let go of the leash!"

It would be so easy to do. Megan would understand. He would tell her everything.

But a vision of Jayden, curled up in the dark on the muddy bank of the Salmon River, flashed into Charlie's mind. Maybe somebody, somewhere, needed help. What if ...? He didn't know how to formulate the rest of the question. Just, *what if*?

Charlie sprinted behind Buster, skidding on the slick grass.

The barbed wire fence that surrounded the equestrian centre loomed.

It was now or never. Lungs screaming, he packed on a burst of speed and dived onto Buster's back. The awkward feeling, of legs bouncing uselessly on the wet grass, lasted only a moment before they were airborne. Charlie pulled his legs up and wrapped them carefully around Buster's girth.

His fingers froze instantly. He wished he'd worn gloves. The wind was colder and more piercing than it had been on the ground, and the drizzle penetrated the thin fabric of his jacket. Charlie gritted his teeth to keep them from chattering.

He peered over Buster's shoulder, trying to establish where they were going. Buster kept to the same route they'd taken before, straight over the equestrian centre, until they turned and merged with a forested escarpment that ran north-south for several kilometres. Charlie spotted his own neighbourhood to the east, but they stuck to the corridor of trees. Buster clearly did not want to be detected.

Charlie looked straight down. The forest below flew past at dizzying speed. They must have a tailwind, pushing them faster and faster through the wintry air.

Then. For the briefest of moments, the world stood still, and they dropped. Straight down. Charlie's stomach lurched. The darkness below reached up for them. Then, as suddenly, they were churning forward again. An air pocket. Charlie's breath came in ragged gasps. He shifted his weight forward and clung.

When he opened his eyes, he saw a ribbon of taillights on Fraser Highway, as he and Buster flew south.

Buster's pace was steady, his nose pointed straight ahead. There was something very determined about his relentless surging.

It came to Charlie with the force of a pickup truck landing on his head. Due south. The border.

They were going back to the international boundary between the United States and Canada. The place where they'd seen the mysterious campfire.

Charlie scanned the sky. No sign of American fighter jets. Yet.

Chapter 19

SMOKE

Buster began his descent.

It was like the time they flew to Hawaii when Dad had a conference. The sound of the engines changed, and the plane felt like it was tipping forward. It was the same now, only no plane and no engines.

Charlie peered ahead. Nothing but thick black darkness—the endless line of forest that marked the border between the two countries. Every little while, a faint shimmer of light glinted off the eerie white obelisks that marked the boundary. Charlie remembered asking Dad, one time, about the pointy metallic posts that stood every mile or so along Zero Avenue.

With the cold biting through his jacket, he pressed himself tighter against Buster's body.

Then, down they went, banking wide at first, but gradually narrowing the circle. Charlie leaned out, studying the landscape below, as they skimmed the tops of the trees. At this height, he picked up the first telltale smell of smoke.

Buster circled again. Right below them, an obelisk glowed in the light from a streetlight on Zero Avenue, and right beside it stood a baby fir tree, the perfect size and shape for a Christmas tree.

Charlie searched the darkness for firelight. He could smell smoke and imagine the glowing embers down below him somewhere. Had someone seen them and doused the flames?

Buster was flying so slowly now, that Charlie's chest tightened with fear at the thought that they might lose their momentum and plummet. He squeezed his eyes closed, pushing away the image of being torn apart by branches if he fell to earth.

When he opened his eyes again, he saw it. The tiniest opening in the trees and, below it, a clearing. Patches of shadow clumped together, but there was no movement. The wood smoke was strongest here.

"Buster!" Charlie hissed into the dog's ear. "We have to get out of here. I can't see what's going on, but I have a bad feeling somebody down there can see us."

Buster turned his head, sending a drizzle of dog saliva onto Charlie's cheek. Then he veered sharply and lunged headlong up and away.

Charlie grasped the thick ruff of Buster's shoulder fur, to keep from sliding back onto the dog's haunches. For endless seconds, they angled upward until, finally, Buster levelled off. Charlie gulped in lungfuls of cold air, and wondered how long he'd stopped breathing. Bit by bit, he relaxed his grip on Buster's fur, a wave of relief washing over him. They were headed back to the clinic.

But. It hit him with a dull thud. The clinic would be locked and deserted. He was getting used to that. How was he going to get home? He'd forgotten he hadn't come by bike. And there were two things he knew absolutely. If he walked home, he'd never make it in time to go to Samir's. And, in any case, Mom would have killed him, so it wouldn't matter, anyway.

Charlie scanned the landscape below and tried to get his bearings. They were already approaching Fraser Highway—temptingly close to home.

"So, Buster," he whispered into the dog's ear. "You've met my mom. What do you think she'd do if I had to bring you home, just this once?"

Buster kept a steady pace.

"I'll take that as a yes," Charlie said.

That was that, then. Two out of the three concerned were in favour. What was the worst that could happen? Now the question was, how to tell Buster about the new destination.

Charlie shifted his weight forward, leaned out, and pointed. "Right down there. That's my street—the one that's like the letter T, with a dead end either way. Go Buster! Go down there. Home, Buster!"

Buster slowed down and treaded air.

Charlie pointed again. "Good boy," he encouraged.

Buster altered course and began a steep descent.

Charlie saw Samir's house first, right at the end of the cul-de-sac. All the lights were on.

Buster steered their flight over the backyards, keeping to the ravine behind the houses.

Charlie pointed again to his own house, just four doors along from Samir's on the other side of the street. "That one," he said.

They landed off-balance, behind the compost box at the end of the yard. Charlie flopped onto his back and lay panting.

Buster gave Charlie's face a quick lick and started toward the house.

"Wait up," Charlie whispered. "I've gotta think about how to do this."

But Buster's toenails were already making a clicking sound on the back steps. Then he scratched at the kitchen door before Charlie could stop him.

Mom opened the door and looked out, clearly puzzled by the noise. Then she looked down to where Buster stood, waiting expectantly, his sides heaving and drool pooling at his feet.

She stood speechless for a moment, staring at the dog, her mouth twisted up to the side. "Hello, Buster," she said finally. "I've been wondering when you were going to show up here."

Chapter 20

THE THIN EDGE

The lies came tumbling out.

"I had to, Mom. I didn't have my bike because I got a flat, and Nick gave me a ride, so we started out for a walk, and then I thought about how I'd be late getting home again, and miss dinner, and that it made more sense just to walk home. With Buster." Charlie studied Mom's face, trying to gauge her reaction. "Can he stay, just tonight? Or maybe the weekend? He's a really good dog, and he's so lonely, and he's used to being outside, so he won't even bother your allergies."

Mom squinted, a sign she was thinking hard.

He tried to look pathetic. Maybe the fact that Dad was gone would work in his favour. "He doesn't have to come in. I'll build him a pen in the back. Please. I'll do the dishes every day for a week."

Mom sighed. "This is not a good idea," she said.

"But he's so lonely and ..." Charlie began.

"What about Dr. Anderton? You'd have to let him know."

"Absolutely," said Charlie. "I think he'll be happy for Buster."

"Well ... just for the weekend," said Mom. She looked tired, like she didn't have the energy to fight. "But don't be thinking this is the thin edge of the wedge. This is an exception."

Buster thumped his tail.

"And you, old fellow," she said, wagging her finger at Buster. "Don't you be looking at me with those big sad eyes." She turned back into the kitchen and closed the door.

Buster leaned into Charlie's leg.

Charlie bent down and scratched his ears. "You never know," he said. "It *could* be the thin edge of the wedge."

Mom opened the door again. "Samir phoned. I said you'd call him back. Apparently, you're sleeping over." She shook her head like this was all too much to cope with.

Charlie winced and scrunched up his face. One more little fib. Special circumstances called for drastic measures. "I forgot all about it."

Mom looked down at Buster. "He's not coming in the house." She didn't quite slam the door, but it closed with a solid click.

Charlie whooped as he pounded down the stairs, Buster at his heels. "This is totally the thin edge of the wedge. You can stay!" He stopped at the bottom of the steps and knelt down, so he'd have good eye contact. "I'm sorry about the sleepover. If I'd known you'd be here, I never would have said I'd go."

Buster licked inside Charlie's nose.

"Not inside my nose. *On* is okay. *In* is not okay. Shake?"

Buster lifted his paw.

"Deal." Charlie stood up and surveyed the back of his house. On the ground level, a sliding door opened onto a concrete patio. He walked over, pushed the sliding door open, and switched on the outdoor light.

He studied the patio. On one side, there was a wooden retaining wall. On the other side, Dad had put up a trellis, so Mom's sweet peas had something to climb. All he'd have to do was build a barrier across the fourth side, and he'd have a pen for Buster. He'd use the boards stacked at the side of the house, the ones they used to build bike jumps.

Charlie felt a wave of self-pity wash over him. It'd be pretty easy to do if Dad were here. He bent down and clipped Buster's leash to the trellis.

"Need help?"

Charlie looked up, quickly swiping at his eyes with the sleeve of his jacket. Mark was just inside the sliding door, pulling on his shoes. He already had the toolbox. It had to be a setup. His brother wasn't that angelic. He probably wanted something.

Mark laughed. "You need to close your mouth or a bat's gonna fly in. Don't worry. I haven't lost my mind. Mom sent me."

Ah. Good. Not so suspicious. And no ulterior motive. "I'll get the wood."

Together, it took them three trips to haul the boards from the side of the house to the back.

Mark grabbed a can of nails he'd left just inside the door. "So, what's the plan?" he asked.

"I'm just going to nail up boards between these two posts. Should be pretty straightforward." This was going to be so much easier with Mark's help.

"How's he going to get out?"

Charlie pulled out the longest board from the pile

they'd made, and laid it across the opening. "I guess I could lift him over?"

Mark jabbed his finger in Buster's direction. "You're going to lift *him*?"

They turned and studied the dog.

Buster was sitting on his haunches, swishing his tail back and forth over the concrete.

"Right," Mark said, starting to pull a sheet of plywood from the pile. "He probably weighs about ninety pounds. Why don't we just make the bottom piece into a kind of gate you can swing up when you want to let him out?"

"That'd work." Charlie eyed his brother. It was kind of fishy, how nice everyone was being to him.

◆

Mom stepped out onto the patio, just as they hammered in the last nail. She held up a mini Spiderman sleeping bag. "You can give him this."

"Cool," Charlie said. "Where'd that come from?"

"The baby box. I've been meaning to recycle it. But you'd better put some newspapers underneath to keep out the damp. Supper's in five."

Later, sitting around the table with Mark and Mom, Charlie kept one ear open for Buster, but the dog seemed to know what he had to do. Charlie cut into his meatloaf and felt guilty. Buster would have loved meatloaf.

"You'll need to make sure he has water," Mom said.

"Done. He's got a whole bucket."

"What about food?"

Charlie lowered his gaze. "Taken care of." He could feel both Mark and Mom staring at him.

"What food?" Mom pressed. "When did you get him food?"

"Yeah, Charlie," Mark said, "what food?"

Charlie squirmed. He knew it wasn't ideal. "Cornflakes," he said stuffing mashed potatoes into his mouth. "With milk."

Chapter 21

BARKING IN THE NIGHT

Charlie hopped from foot to foot at the back door, waiting for Mom to run through her checklist of all the things he might have forgotten.

She folded her arms over her chest. "Toothbrush?"

"Of course." He eyed the clock. Another minute and he'd be officially late.

"A book to read?"

Charlie's head jerked up. "Pu—leez."

"What about Buster?"

She was right, of course. It was crazy to spend the night at Samir's when he only had Buster for the weekend. But he'd promised, and a promise was a promise. Besides, he'd been such a hermit lately, he was relieved that Samir still wanted to do stuff. He squared his shoulders and tried to sound responsible. "He's got water. I've taken him out for a pee. I'm two minutes away if I need to come home in a hurry."

"This is not how I imagined spending my Friday night." Mom looked like she might cry.

"Trust me, Mom. He'll be fine. And if he's not, you can call me."

"And tomorrow, we have to get him proper food."

He held Mom's gaze. "I know. The cornflakes were just a snack, so he'd feel like he was part of the family." It took all his willpower not to tell her he hadn't wanted to upset her by raiding the cupboard for proper food.

He'd just finished tying his shoes when Mom made an unexpected lunge, grabbing his head with both hands and planting a warm kiss on his forehead. "Have fun," she said.

Charlie wiped the kiss off with his sleeve and charged down the steps two at a time. At the bottom, he hurried over to Buster's pen.

Buster was on his hind legs, front paws skittering along the top board of the makeshift pen.

Leaning in, Charlie wrapped his arms around Buster. "I'm really sorry," he said. "This isn't how I thought it would be tonight, but I promised Samir, and I can't back out."

Buster panted softly, his breath moist in Charlie's ear.

"The fact is," Charlie continued, "you have to stay. I promise I'll be back first thing in the morning." He tried to make his voice sound firm, but inside, he felt like he was abandoning his best friend.

Buster dropped to all fours, furrowing his brow. He retreated to the corner of the pen, circled twice on the Spiderman sleeping bag, and then flopped down where he could still gaze at Charlie.

"Good dog, Buster." Charlie's heart was heavy as he set off, up the broken sidewalk beside his house. He trudged the short distance to Samir's house at the end of the street, hoping Buster would understand and forgive him for leaving. He was definitely "stuck between a rock and a hard place," as Dad used to say.

Charlie was surprised that it was Samir's dad who answered the door. He was a long-haul trucker, and most Fridays he was still on the road. He was a big man, the kind of man who looked like he might own a trucking company. But it was Samir's mom who owned the company, at least that's what Mr. Grewal said. Charlie could never tell if he was joking or not.

"Charlie," he stated, eyeing the plastic bag in Charlie's

hand. "Have you run away from home?" Behind him, Samir's mom waved him in.

Charlie swallowed against the lump that formed in his throat. A mom and dad. Together. In the same house. "Hey, Mr. Grewal," he said. "Just for the night."

Samir appeared at the top of the stairs. "What took you so long? Did you have to do surgery again?"

Charlie rolled his eyes. "Better than that. I got to bring Buster home."

"Lucky," Samir said, then added louder, so his mom would hear. "Charlie gets to have a dog!"

"Not to keep," Charlie explained. "At least, not yet. But I'm working on it."

Samir started down the stairs. "Come on. I want to meet him."

Charlie hesitated. "How about after your game tomorrow? I've got him all settled in for the night, and I don't want to stir things up. Mom's a little touchy about him being there, and I don't want to throw off my chances of Buster making a good impression."

Samir looked like he was going to insist.

Charlie took charge. He turned back to Samir's mom and dad. "Thanks for having me over," he said.

Then he bounded up the carpeted stairs to meet Samir, who was halfway down.

"I get the silver controller," he said, dumping his plastic bag on the lower bunk, and plunking himself down on the floor beside the bed. "Game on."

In seconds, Charlie was focussed on the screen, vaguely conscious of the smell of sweaty socks in Samir's bedroom. He pushed his brain to think about obliterating zombies, and weaving his avatar through gloomy medieval streets, dodging laser fire. But mostly, all he could think about was Buster, curled up all by himself on the Spiderman bedding. He should never have left him alone.

Much later, almost two o'clock by the red glow of Samir's clock, Charlie still wasn't asleep. He ached to be with Buster. Every time he closed his eyes, he was in the air on Buster's back, the icy bite of a cloudless night stinging his face. Samir snored softly, dead to the world, but Charlie couldn't stop remembering the feeling of flying and the smell of campfire smoke. No matter how hard he tried, he couldn't turn off his brain.

Samir's bedroom window was open a crack, and the venetian blind bumped softly against the windowsill.

The chilly air coming in reminded Charlie of the sharp cold of his dusk flights. He shivered and turned away from the window.

Then he heard it. First, a volley of deep barks. Then it went quiet. Then the barks again, followed by a broken howl. Charlie sat up and put his ear to the open window, trying to locate the bark. Which of the neighbourhood dogs would be barking at this hour?

It had to be Buster. Charlie had never actually heard him bark, but there was no other dog it could be.

He glanced over at Samir. What to do? Mom would hear the racket soon, if she hadn't already, but she wouldn't phone Samir's house in the middle of the night.

Charlie groped in the darkness for his jeans. He was pretty sure he'd left his jacket with his runners by the front door. He hoped Samir's mom hadn't put them away.

He tiptoed the length of the hall and crept down the stairs. He felt his jacket at the bottom of the banister, and spotted his runners neatly placed, just inside the front hall closet. He picked them up and froze. Someone was moving upstairs. A door closed. He waited, heart hammering. The silence flooded back. He turned the dead bolt slowly to the left.

The bolt made a loud clunk as it opened. Charlie tensed, then pushed the door open and closed it softly behind him. He stood on the step and pulled on his shoes, cast a guilty glance at the door he was leaving unlocked, and bounded for the street. He prayed none of the neighbours would just happen to be looking out their window, and mistake him for a burglar running through the night.

He ran past the three houses between his place and Samir's, and cut diagonally across his own yard, straight for the patio at the back. The dew was already heavy on the grass. He could feel the cold and wet coming through his runners. The barking had stopped.

Buster was standing on his hind legs, front paws pressed on the topmost board of his kennel.

"What's wrong? It's the middle of the night!"

Buster stretched forward and licked Charlie's face. His dark eyes flashed.

Charlie felt prickles at the back of his neck. He scanned the house for any sign of lights or movement. Nothing.

"Okay, fella, hang on." He pulled the bottom board up and Buster shimmied out.

Buster started to trot, nose straight ahead, and tail stretched out behind. He stopped, his dark silhouette just visible in the faint glow from the streetlight, one forepaw poised in mid-air. "Are you coming or not?" his body seemed to say.

"It has to be now?" Charlie whispered. But he knew the answer. Someone was in trouble. He glanced back at the dark house. "Okay. I'm coming."

Buster was almost at the compost bin.

Charlie sprinted down the yard and leapt.

Chapter 22

FIRELIGHT

They became airborne at the precise moment of contact.

"Yes," Charlie whispered into the fur at Buster's neck. No dragging his knees in the dirt. "Perfect takeoff. Good boy."

Buster's legs churned in a powerful rhythm as they cleared the tops of the trees and veered over Samir's house.

Charlie let go the breath he'd been holding, relieved that all was in darkness. In the distance, the lights of downtown Langley twinkled under a clear, dark sky. Charlie knew, without a shadow of a doubt, that tonight, he would know the story of the mysterious campfire. He pulled the sleeves of his jacket down over his bare hands. In the sky, it was already winter.

Buster turned his head a little to the side, looking back at Charlie out of the corner of his eye.

And Charlie knew what Buster was telling him: "We're in this together. It'll be okay."

Charlie laid his cheek against the dog's warm neck, and tried not to look down. "Easy for you to say," he mumbled. Already his legs ached with the effort of keeping them hugged up around Buster's middle, and his fingers tingled from the cold.

He raised his head again, forcing himself to look.

It was like before. Buster kept to the forested escarpment. No houses. No lights. Behind them, red taillights, even in the middle of night, dotted the highway. Ahead, wide-open empty fields lay like a checkerboard, in shades of charcoal and black.

Charlie had guessed right. They were approaching the border.

Below them, the uninhabited forest that ran east-west along the boundary stretched like a black velvet band, as far he could see in either direction. Streetlights along Zero Avenue cast an eerie blue light that collected in puddles on the empty pavement.

Buster slowed, easing them down, until they were barely skimming the trees. The nighttime smell of sleeping forest filled Charlie's nose.

Buster banked in a tight curve, his nose pointing forward and down.

Then Charlie caught it—the smell of campfire smoke. And, at the same moment, he glimpsed a flicker of flames below them.

A shudder broke like an electrical shock through Buster's body. For one terrifying moment, he pawed the air. Then, without warning, he dove sharply, narrowly missing the black outstretched branches of a Douglas fir.

It was their worst landing yet. Charlie pitched off Buster's side, sprawling against the trunk of a tree. He lay for a minute, struggling to catch his breath, and waiting for his eyes to adjust to the darkness.

Buster was a few feet away. He had flattened himself into the forest floor and, even though his sides were heaving, his panting made no sound at all.

Charlie held his breath and listened.

Buster began to inch forward on his belly, until he was lying so close, they were touching. His dark brown eyes locked onto Charlie's.

Charlie wished for the millionth time that Buster could talk. If only Charlie knew what he was supposed to do next. Buster expected something.

A vision of Jayden, waving from his mom's arms, flashed like an ad across Charlie's brain. Someone was in trouble. It was up to him now. He glanced again at Buster. The dog's teeth glinted, even in the dark.

"What now?" he whispered.

Buster butted Charlie's shoulder with his nose.

Charlie squinted. Through the trees, he could just make out the dance of firelight. He crept forward on his hands and knees.

Buster edged along, too, silent and warm at his side. Inch by inch, they gained ground.

Charlie could see there was a little clearing in the trees, where the campfire was. But a huge stump of what had once been a towering giant of a tree blocked his view.

He pulled himself up, tight against the massive stump, and breathed out. All he had to do was move a few more inches and peek over.

Running his hands over the moss-covered bark, he found a place to grasp.

He looked at Buster. It was now or never.

Buster thumped his tail.

Chapter 23

CAMPERS

There was just enough firelight to see a little settlement.

A log had been pulled up close to the fire, and a man was sitting on it, leaning toward the warmth as close as he could.

Charlie let out his breath, trying to make sense of what he could see. There was a two-man tent, exactly like the one Mom had bought at Bargain Mart, but had eventually thrown out because it leaked.

Just to the side of the tent, a sheet of plastic had been tied up between trees, to make a covered area. Dingy underwear hung from a makeshift clothesline, and two green garbage bags, brimming over with something, lay under the plastic.

Charlie felt the tension in his shoulders release. There was nothing to be afraid of here.

The man didn't look very old. His hair was long and

tangled, and even in the dim light of the campfire, his runners looked wet, his jacket thin and worn.

Charlie swallowed, thinking of the puffy jacket and the waterproof shell he'd got at the start of the school year.

Why was the man here? Was he trying to sneak across the border? But then, why would he set up camp? Maybe he was mentally ill, and couldn't cope with life in the real world. Or drug addicted. But then, he wouldn't stay here. Maybe he was homeless and had nowhere else to go.

Charlie eased himself back down, below the top of the stump.

Buster licked Charlie's eyebrows.

Charlie stared at Buster, thinking hard. Something about their current situation reminded him of a story called "The Shepherd." His family listened to it every Christmas Eve. It was about a Second World War fighter pilot, who gets shot down over the English Channel. But in the years that follow, he returns from his watery grave to guide lost pilots through the fog.

"Is that what you are, Buster?" he whispered into the dog's ear. "Are you like the shepherd, still rescuing people, even when everybody thinks you're too old to be good for much?"

Buster held Charlie's gaze, his tail thumping.

A foul smell floated into the air between them.

"Braghhh." Charlie screwed up his face. "At a time like this," he mouthed, "you fart?" He leaned back against the stump.

Buster shimmied closer, so their bodies were touching again.

Charlie put his arm around Buster's shoulders. "I think you *are* like the shepherd," he whispered. "You brought us this far. But now I think it's up to me."

A sharp cry pierced the silence of the forest.

Charlie froze, listening, but there were no other sounds.

He shifted onto his knees, pulling himself up, so he could see over the top of the stump. The tent flap opened. A woman struggled out, one arm clutching a baby, the other grasping the edge of the tent to keep her balance. She stood up and half-stumbled toward the fire.

Charlie stared. She could have been Mark's girl-friend, she was so young. She had on jeans and a dark hoodie. Her hair was pulled back in a long ponytail. She bounced the baby up and down in her arms, her whole body shaking with the effort. The baby howled.

The man stood up and moved away from the log to give the woman a space to sit down. And that was when Charlie noticed the man's limp. His face twisted with the pain, every time he put weight on his leg.

Charlie strained to hear what they were saying, but their voices were low, and the baby's howl drowned them out.

"... just can't get him to sleep ... diapers ... if only I could ..."

The man poked the fire, sending a puff of sparks into the air. "I know," he said. "... water for the milk powder ..."

The woman dropped her head over the baby in her arms. Her shoulders shook.

Charlie slid back down behind the stump. This family was homeless. He'd seen the stories in the newspaper. They'd talked about it at school. He knew about people living on the street. But it was different when you saw it up close. The baby was hungry, and the guy was hurt.

He had to do something. But he couldn't just walk in and say hi. They were camped here for a reason. He could call the police. But that might get them in trouble. They weren't trying to hurt anyone. Something terrible must have happened to them, and there was the baby, and the man was injured, and they couldn't get food and whatever else they needed.

But Charlie could do that. He could at least get them food and warmer clothes, until he figured out what else to do.

He took Buster's face between his hands. "We're going back to get supplies. We're no good to them here."

Buster stood up and shook.

Ducking the spray of slobber, Charlie hunched down, and tiptoed away from the ring of firelight and through the wet underbrush, until he saw the white obelisk marking the Canadian side of the border. Beyond it, Zero Avenue stretched into the distance, black and empty at this hour.

Buster trotted ahead, picking up speed as they approached open space.

Charlie zipped up his jacket, scanned the darkness around them, and began to run. He caught Buster's ruff at the point of liftoff. They were getting to be so good at this.

Charlie glanced back over his shoulder. In the darkness of the endless forest, there was no sign of the campfire, and the sound of the baby's crying was lost in the rush of wind past his ears.

He hitched his legs up and tightened his grip. "Home," he ordered.

But Buster was almost there.

Chapter 24

THINGS THAT GO BUMP IN THE NIGHT

They touched down in the slimy mud behind the compost bin. Charlie picked himself up, gagging at the smell of rotten leaves and vegetables. He tried to wipe the muddy smears from his pants.

Buster lay on the grass, sides heaving, his breath forming clouds of condensation in the cool night air.

"You okay?" Charlie bent down and rubbed his soft back. "Take a minute to get your breath. It's okay."

Buster heaved himself to his feet and leaned against Charlie's legs.

"Come on," Charlie encouraged. "Let's get you back to bed. That's enough excitement for one night."

Buster plodded up the lawn behind Charlie.

Charlie held up the lower board while Buster wriggled through, heading straight for the sleeping bag, not even taking the time to circle twice, before flopping down.

"Go back to sleep," Charlie whispered.

But Buster's head was already down, his eyes closed.

Charlie sneaked across the yard, looking up at the dark windows. Mom would freak if she heard noises outside in the middle of the night. He shivered. It would be different if Dad was there.

Keeping to the shadow of the hedges, where the streetlights didn't penetrate the darkness, Charlie hurried back to Samir's. He took his shoes off at the bottom of the front steps and tiptoed softly up to the door.

He reached for the knob, dreading the possibility that someone had discovered it open and locked it. He eased the door ajar, with only a low, hollow click of the latch. He set his shoes down where Samir's mom had placed them earlier, and started up the stairs.

He edged slowly upward, stopping after each creak to listen. He was halfway to the top, when he had the prickly sensation of being watched. He checked behind him. Nothing. When he reached the landing, he looked up. There was Samir, silhouetted in the ghostly light from the streetlight outside. He was in his boxers, standing in the hallway, legs wide apart, a baseball bat poised and ready to swing.

"It's me," Charlie hissed. "What's with the baseball bat?"

Samir lowered the bat, waiting until Charlie reached the top of the stairs. "I'm going out to hit a few balls, what do you think?" he hissed back. "What are *you* doing? I thought you were a burglar."

Charlie was suddenly exhausted. He felt like a balloon someone had stabbed with a pin. His legs ached and he was cold right through. "It's a long story," he whispered.

They crept noiselessly down the hall to Samir's room. Samir closed the door, and came and sat beside Charlie on the lower bunk. "So, do you want to tell me about it, or take your chances with the bat?"

Charlie bit his lip. The last thing in the world he wanted to do was tell anybody about Buster. It was too unbelievable. Samir would think he'd lost his mind and tell Mom. He would never get to keep Buster. He'd probably be put in a program for people with delusional thinking, and Buster would go to that couple who'd been asking Dr. Anderton about him. Or not.

On the other hand, it would be a relief to tell somebody. And Samir *was* his best friend. They'd been keeping each other's secrets since they were six.

He took a deep breath. He opened his mouth. He almost started to tell the truth. But then he thought— what if Buster wouldn't fly for anyone else, and Samir didn't believe him? He might never get back to the family by the campfire. He couldn't take that chance.

"I had to go get Buster. Didn't you hear him barking?"

Samir looked doubtful. "I didn't hear anything, until I heard what I thought was a burglar down by the front door."

"Well, he was barking like crazy, and I figured he'd wake Mom, and she'd phone here and wake everybody up, so I had to go settle him down."

Samir rolled the bat under the bed. "You scared the crap out of me." He climbed up into the top bunk. "How'd you get him to stop barking?"

Charlie thought fast. "I took him for a little walk around the yard. He had to pee. I also gave him half a Caramilk bar I found in my pocket. He liked that a lot."

Samir grunted. "A Caramilk? Aren't you afraid he'll get cavities?"

Charlie punched his pillow. A Caramilk? Where had that come from? He didn't even like Caramilk. Besides, he knew for sure, chocolate was bad for dogs.

"Anyway. That wasn't really a long story." Samir's words were almost lost in a yawn.

Charlie caught Samir's yawn. "Condensed version," he said. He rolled over, snuggling into the warmth of the covers.

Through the slats in the blind, he could see a sliver of moon sliding silently over the tops of the trees. He thought about the border, the longest unmanned border in the world. All darkness and trees and empty space. He saw the boundary markers glimmering eerily white. It was just an imaginary line. Anyone could walk across it. Or smuggle something across it. Is that what he had stumbled on? Was the family involved in smuggling, just waiting for their connection to arrive?

Charlie fell into a fitful sleep. But even in his sleep, he knew the sad family clinging together in the cold was not involved in smuggling.

Chapter 25

THE BORDER

Charlie smelled coffee. And bacon. And something burning. Pancakes? He thumped his feet against the top bunk, but getting no response, he stretched up to look. Samir's covers were on the floor and his bed was empty.

When he swung his legs out of bed, his muscles protested. He stared at his bare toes, thinking about the possibility that it had all been a dream. But no, the evidence was there—his jeans were in a heap beside the bed, the knees still wet and muddy. He pulled them on, cringing when the slimy fabric touched his skin. He thought about the family camping at the border. There would be no bacon for them this morning. How could he help them? He needed a plan.

He was partway down the stairs when he thought of Samir's parents. They ran a trucking company. Samir's dad did long hauls, lots of times to the States. If anybody knew about crossing the border, Mr. Grewal would.

Charlie entered the bright kitchen through a smoky haze.

Samir's dad had opened the French doors onto the deck and was flapping his newspaper, trying to clear the air. "Don't mind all this smoke."

"Morning, Charlie." Samir's mom looked up from scraping a pan full of pancakes into the compost bin, and glared at her husband. "Too many distractions. I lost track of this batch, but there's a stack ready to go in the oven. Entirely Mr. Grewal's fault."

"Morning." Charlie slid into his usual chair. "Where's Samir?"

"Here." Samir emerged from the den, the TV remote still in his hand. He was already dressed for soccer.

Charlie's gut clenched at the sight of the uniform. Maybe he'd made a mistake, quitting soccer. But with Dad gone, his heart wasn't in it.

Samir sat down next to Charlie. "You're finally up. That was quite the night."

Charlie nodded. He didn't want to talk about it, at least not in front of Samir's parents. He was grateful

Samir's mom descended on them with the hot platter of pancakes.

"Help yourself," she said, smacking Samir's hand back. "Company first."

"Charlie's not company, he's Charlie."

"Still," she said, returning to the stove.

Charlie helped himself. He watched the syrup curl out of the bottle, thinking about how he could get Mr. Grewal to talk about the border. It wasn't like he usually had long conversations with Samir's dad. It might be weird if he started now.

But he had to.

"So, Mr. Grewal, how's work these days?"

Samir's mom and dad turned their heads and stared at him.

Charlie blushed.

Mr. Grewal set down his newspaper. "Well, how thoughtful of you to ask. Work is fine, thank you." He leaned closer to Charlie. "Has your mother been sending you to charm school?"

Samir's mom dropped another batch of pancakes onto the platter. "Charlie doesn't need to go to charm school. He's always been charming. It comes naturally."

Charlie stuffed his mouth with pancakes, careful to keep the syrup from dripping on his pants.

"Although," Mr. Grewal continued, "I have to say, I particularly like work when it's the weekend and I'm not doing it."

Charlie wracked his brain. He had to keep him talking. "Do you get more business now that there's free trade with the U.S.?"

Mr. Grewal took a long swig of his coffee and set his mug down.

Charlie could see he was trying not to smile.

"It depends what you're hauling. For a lot of guys, there are probably some changes, but for us, it's always pretty steady."

"Do you have to line up at the border, like we do when we go to the States?"

"Oh, yeah. There's a separate lane for trucks, but you still get lineups." He raised his eyebrows at Charlie.

Charlie needed more. "So, don't you sometimes wish you knew some old back road you could take, so you could cross the border without all that hassle?"

Samir's mom turned from the stove and studied Charlie.

Mr. Grewal got up and refilled his mug. "My rig's too big for any old back road, like you're talking about. But, in any case, I wouldn't ever want to tangle with the border patrol."

"There's a border patrol?"

"You bet. On both sides. The Americans have a whole fleet of border vehicles, some of them marked and some of them unmarked. They're cruising along those back roads all the time. And the Canadians. We've got a little different system, but we've got our border patrols out there watching things."

"But don't you think they could miss something? Like, if you were careful and knew what you were doing, don't you think it would be possible to smuggle something or someone across the border and not get caught?"

"Well, I wouldn't be the one to try it. The patrols might miss you, but they've got sensors and surveillance helicopters. They've even got spies. You can wander for miles along the slash, but step over the line, and you're on their radar."

Samir choked on his orange juice. "No way. Spies?"

"Don't kid yourself. They've got spies. And I tell you, I wouldn't want to get picked up by a border guy. You'd be catching up on your reading, in a federal jail, before you knew what hit you."

"So, what's the *slash*?" Charlie felt like he might be getting somewhere.

"Twenty feet. Ten on either side of the line. Twenty open feet they keep mowed and logged, from one side of the continent to the other. Shows up on satellite pictures."

Samir's mom sat down and leaned in, with her elbows on the table, the flipper poised in the air. "Thinking of heading south?"

Charlie helped himself to another pancake. "No. I just wonder about it. I still think it might be possible. They can't keep track of the whole border all the time. I bet if you're a real criminal, you could figure out when the patrols come by and find a way through."

"It happens. We're talking about the longest unmanned border between two countries in the world. If somebody wants to come through that border, or bring something through without checking in with customs, they can do it. It's possible and it happens. But you'd be taking a huge risk." Mr. Grewal waggled his finger at Charlie. "I wouldn't recommend it."

Charlie was so full he could hardly breathe. He

pushed his last bite of pancake around the syrup on his plate and thought about the pathetic family he and Buster had found. What were they having for breakfast?

"So, what's happening, Charlie?" Samir's dad picked up his paper and hovered in the doorway. "Are you planning on skipping the country, or is it some smuggling you've got in mind?"

Charlie laughed. "Neither. I've just always wondered about it, and you seemed like the guy to ask."

Charlie carried his plate to the sink. So. That family had to be homeless. Not smugglers or even refugees. They couldn't have crossed the border. They would have been picked up long before now, if they'd actually crossed the slash and stepped across that invisible line. They were just a little family, trying to exist in a hidden corner of the forest, where nobody would bother them.

It was the saddest thing ever.

He followed Samir upstairs to get his stuff. By the time he got to the top stair, he had a plan.

Chapter 26

OPERATION FEED THE HOMELESS

It was a plan with many steps, but by the time Charlie reached his own driveway, he had it down to three main ones:

1. Fix his flat tire.
2. Gather some food and blankets and anything else he could think of.
3. Deliver the stuff to the family.

It wasn't the best of plans. He knew that. The family needed real help, not just a quick fix. But it would take him more time to figure out how to make that happen. He didn't want them to get in trouble for camping on the border. And he definitely didn't want anyone to take away their baby. All he wanted was to make sure they had enough to eat, and some warm gear, until he had a better plan. It was a start.

The driveway was empty. So far, so good. He looked

at his watch. Mark would be at work already, and Mom always did the grocery shopping Saturday morning, and then had lunch with her sister. The coast was clear, but he had to act fast.

First, Buster. Happy he'd remembered his key, he unlocked the front door and dropped his pack. The house still smelled like fried onions.

Buster barked, three loud woofs and then silence, as if he was listening.

"I'm coming!" Charlie raced downstairs and out through the sliding door.

Buster leapt up, knocking Charlie off balance, and landing with his front paws on Charlie's chest.

Charlie leaned back against the sliding door, and closed his eyes and mouth against the frenzy of dog kisses. "Who's the good boy?" he said. "Okay, okay, Buster. That's enough with the licking. We've got work to do." Charlie scrambled to his feet and pulled up the bottom board, watching as Buster bounded into the backyard and did his morning business.

Buster sniffed suspiciously at the corner of the fence, where the neighbour's cat sometimes watched for birds.

"I'll be right there with your breakfast," Charlie yelled, and raced back up to the kitchen.

He pulled open the fridge door. Tucked behind the platter with the leftover meatloaf, he found what he'd been hoping for. Three sausages and mashed potatoes from Thursday. If Mark hadn't scarfed them by now, they were fair game.

He grabbed the container, and shot downstairs and out through the patio doors.

Buster abandoned his inspection of the backyard and loped back to the house to watch Charlie spoon the food into his dish. He started to eat, and then changed his mind, and slopped up half the water in his bucket.

"Not exactly dog food, but better than cornflakes," Charlie said. He sat down on Buster's bedding, and watched him wolf down the rest of his breakfast, sausages first, then the potatoes.

Buster licked the bowl clean, scraping it across the patio until he'd got every last bit. Then he flopped down beside Charlie, laying his head on his lap.

Charlie scratched his ears, wondering what he'd have to do to convince Mom to let him stay. Buster had already proven he could handle being outside.

And Charlie would have to work fast. The couple that had shown interest was coming back next week to take another look.

"There's still hope," he whispered. "We have to keep up the pressure." He stood up. "Come on, Buster. Let's go fix my flat. You can't perform a rescue if you don't have wheels." He pushed his face forward for Buster to lick. "Well, I guess you could, but I'm going to need my bike to get some food down to that family."

Charlie rummaged through the toolbox in the garage. When he'd found what he thought he'd need, he flipped his bike upside down, like he'd seen Dad do.

Buster curled up to watch in a patch of sunlight.

Charlie'd never changed a flat. He'd seen Dad do it. As he surveyed the tools he'd assembled, a dull, angry ache squeezed his chest. Dad should be here to help him.

He kicked the pump and it fell over with a clatter.

Buster struggled to his feet, looking up at Charlie expectantly.

Charlie sighed. "I know. Fix the tire."

It took forever. He used the plastic tire levers to get the tire off. It looked easy when Dad did it, but it took Charlie endless minutes, just to figure out how to slip the levers under the rubber, and pull the tire away from the rim. Then he had to find the cause of the flat. That was easier. It was a staple, both ends jabbed through the tube.

Charlie looked at his watch and winced. Half the morning had slipped away. He rummaged through the patch kit, remembering what Dad had shown him— put glue on both surfaces, and wait till it got tacky, before you pressed the patch down onto the tube.

Who would have thought it would take so long to fix a flat? He wished Dad were here.

Or did he? All those nights when he could hear them arguing downstairs, but could never hear what they were arguing about. All the pretending that everything was okay.

He attached the pump to the valve and shifted it around, until he could see the gauge.

He didn't think he'd ever get it pumped up to ninety PSI. It took way longer than when Dad did it. By the time he'd finished, he was in a sweat. He smelled his pits. "Phew," he said.

He pressed down on the tire. It felt about right. He put his ear to the rubber and listened for a hiss. The air stayed in.

"Ta da!" he said, and flipped the bike right side up. He wheeled it out to the driveway. There was no sign of Mom's car.

He checked his watch again. Almost noon.

Buster was curled up beside the lawn mower, showing no signs of getting up.

"You stay," Charlie ordered. Then he raced inside and pulled two green garbage bags out of the box under the kitchen sink. He headed to the spare room in the basement, where all the junk that might be useful someday was piled up. The musty smell caught in his nose even before he flicked on the light. He knew he'd seen blankets in the closet, but he had to smile when he saw them. Spaceman quilts. Two of them. He and Mark had both had one. He stuffed them into the garbage bags.

The box of old things for the Salvation Army was kept in the same room. Charlie's heart lurched when he opened it. Dad's old sweaters. Just like that. Out with Dad. Out with the old sweaters.

He chose three. They smelled like Dad—the Irish Spring soap that Mom hated the smell of, and wouldn't allow in the powder room that was supposed to be for company.

Then he checked the freezer. He pulled out two bags of hamburger buns. His hand hovered over a loaf of raisin bread. Mom probably wouldn't notice. He slipped the raisin bread into the bag.

On his way through the kitchen, he grabbed a bag of oranges, a package of cheese, and a box of granola bars. He pulled the bulging bags out to the garage.

Buster yawned and stretched out his rear end, then his front legs. Then he followed Charlie out to the driveway.

"What do you think," said Charlie. "Where shall I put them?"

Buster plodded across the grass and found a stick in a flower bed. He stared at it expectantly.

"Give me one sec," Charlie said. He scanned the yard. Yes. The front corner where the neighbour's hedge was thickest. They would be out of sight there. He dragged the bags across the lawn.

Buster followed, the stick in his mouth.

"Okay, fella. Time for a little exercise." Charlie picked up the stick, where Buster had dropped it on the grass. "Eww, gross. That's a lot of slobber." He threw the stick in a high arc.

Buster bounded after it, but dropped it partway

back, like he knew something was up. He sat down on his haunches, his eyes riveted on Charlie.

"I have to go out again," Charlie said. He walked across the yard to where the stick lay abandoned, and tossed it again.

Buster watched it sail through the air but didn't move.

"I know," Charlie said, kneeling down.

Buster half-heartedly raised a paw.

"I won't be very long, just as long as it takes to ride down there and deposit the bags of supplies," Charlie explained.

Buster cocked his head to one side.

"Don't look at me like that. You know you couldn't carry all that stuff."

Buster reached up with a hind leg and gave his ear a vigorous scratch.

"It's tricky, though, right?"

Buster whined and swished his tail across the grass.

"I mean, I can ride there. It's not that far. But the reality is, I can't take all that stuff by myself. It won't work."

Buster turned his head toward Samir's house.

Charlie followed his gaze. It was insane. But Buster was right. He needed help. Samir would be home from soccer by now, and, after all, Samir was his best friend. "Come on," he said.

He was flushed with excitement as he bounded up Samir's steps.

Samir came to the door with half a grilled cheese sandwich in his hand. He held it up high as Buster went in for a lick. "Whoa, Buster!" he said kneeling down and scrubbing Buster's head with his free hand. "He's awesome. No wonder you want to keep him." He looked up at Charlie suspiciously. "What's up? No one home to make you lunch?"

"Very funny," Charlie said, eyeing the grilled cheese. "It's not about lunch. I'm on a mission and I need your help."

"Okay." Samir sounded doubtful. "Does that mean you don't want lunch?"

Charlie was salivating.

Samir motioned them in. "Here, you take this one. There's another one in the pan." He reappeared with two half-sandwiches stacked in one hand. "Okay. I'm coming. What do I need?"

"Your bike and a bungee cord."

Samir walked his bike the short distance back to

Charlie's house. He stopped when he spotted the garbage bags, and turned to Charlie. "Is that why I needed a bungee cord?"

Charlie nodded. "They're not that heavy. Just bulky."

Samir squinted at his friend. "How far?"

Charlie bent down and pretended to examine something in Buster's ear. "Not too far," he mumbled. He looked up at Samir, half-afraid he'd be shaking his head.

But Samir shoved the last of his sandwich into his mouth, and wheeled his bike closer to the bags. "You're going to explain it all while we're riding, right?"

"Absolutely."

"What about him?"

"He's not coming."

Buster's ears drooped.

Charlie snagged Buster's collar. "Hang on. I just have to put him in the back."

Charlie lifted the bottom board to let Buster into the pen, and then shimmied in right behind him. He knelt down, and waited for Buster to get settled on the Spiderman sleeping bag. "I guess you don't actually have to stay in there if you don't want to, do you?" he said. Then he lowered his voice. "But it's better if you do. Right? Just for now. Promise to stay."

Buster laid his head on his forepaws and closed his eyes.

Charlie felt he needed to explain. He spelled out the plan, step by step. "Samir and I will get all the stuff down there now. Then you and I will go back tonight and put it where they'll see it. You okay with that?"

Buster opened one eye and crossed his front paws. In the deep shade at the back of the house, the white whiskers around his muzzle stood out.

Charlie's voice was soft. "It's not that far, but it's too far for you to come with us. On foot, I mean. It's not good for a dog to run alongside a bike. Too dangerous, and not the kind of running dogs are supposed to do." He reached down and gave Buster's head a gentle rub with his knuckles—a lot softer than the noogies his brother gave Charlie. "You and I will fly down later."

Buster opened both eyes.

"I'll be back before you know it. Trust me," Charlie said. Then he dropped the bottom board into place and sprinted out to the driveway.

Chapter 27

BUT IT'S THE TRUTH

It wasn't far to ride, and at this time of day, even on a Saturday, there were hardly any cars. Charlie flicked on his flashing taillight and motioned for Samir to do the same. It was important, even in the daytime.

It was tricky getting started. Charlie's bike wobbled at first, as he clutched the load with one hand to keep it balanced, and gripped the handlebars with the other. He glanced back to see how Samir was doing.

"See," Charlie said, when Samir came alongside him. "It's not so hard, once you get going."

And then Charlie made a decision. It was now or never. He explained everything. About the time he and Buster had found Jayden alone and asleep in the mud by the Salmon River. And about Tyler and the gang of bullies out behind Aldergrove Elementary. He ended with the family huddled in the forest down off Zero Avenue.

He explained it all. All except the part about the flying. He hadn't told Samir about that part, and he knew the question was coming.

Charlie heard a truck approaching from behind and pulled ahead of Samir. Buffeted by the push of air in the truck's wake, he tightened his grip on the garbage bag.

"Geez," Samir complained, spitting out dust. "Could he go any faster?"

Charlie leaned into the handlebars, puffing with the effort of pedalling, while clinging to the bag of supplies. He was still waiting for the question.

Samir pulled alongside again. "So," he started, "you're kind of like Encyclopedia Brown. I always wondered how he found out about all those mysteries. How do you do it, anyway?"

There it was. The question. In his head, he'd tried a hundred ways to explain so it didn't sound like he was losing it.

He blurted it out. "Buster flies me there."

"Right." Samir dropped back to let a car go by. "How, really?"

"That's it. What I said. Buster flies me there. On his back."

"Come on," Samir jeered and sped up. "How do you really find them? Maybe you've just got a natural talent for it, and you'll end up being a real detective or something."

Charlie braked and bumped over onto the gravel shoulder. He waited for Samir to pull up beside him. He looked him right in the eye. "I'm serious. It's not the kind of thing I would make up. The first time it happened, I thought I was in a nightmare, and I felt like I was going to fall the whole time. But now, it's happened so often, I'm kind of getting used to it."

Samir's mouth opened. His lip curled a little, as if he was going to say something sarcastic, but he stopped. No words came out.

"But you can't tell anyone. If you do, they'll probably put me in a program for people with delusional thinking. I mean it, Samir. It's really important you don't tell."

Samir got ready to push off again. "You're such a joker. Duh. In case you didn't know, dogs can't fly."

"Wait," Charlie said, both feet still firmly planted in the gravel. He could hear the panic in his own voice. "It really happened. I didn't imagine it, and I'm not joking."

Samir turned back to Charlie. "Joke's over. It wasn't funny in the first place."

"But it's the truth."

Samir stared at Charlie.

"You have to promise not to tell." He could tell he sounded like he was pleading. "Remember when you smoked those cigarettes, and you made me promise not to tell? Well, I didn't. And this is way more serious than that. You have to promise."

Samir's eyes were wide. "Dude," he said. "It's okay. You've been a bit out of it lately. With your dad and everything. I get it." He nodded his head vigorously. "It's really okay."

Charlie's voice was practically a whisper. "But it happened. And you can't tell."

Samir leaned over and gripped Charlie's handlebar. "Then I'm totally going to tell. This is delusional thinking. You need help."

"No! If you tell, I'll never get to keep Buster."

Samir pinched his lips together. "Okay," he said slowly. "I won't tell. But I don't believe you go flying around on a Chocolate Lab named Buster. It's too stupid." He adjusted the bag behind his seat. Then he looked up sharply. "You haven't started taking drugs, have you?"

Charlie made a face. "What do you think?"

Samir gave him an appraising look. "I don't know what

I think, but I definitely don't believe you go flying around the country on Buster. I think maybe you're hallucinating, or you've got fever on the brain or something."

Charlie leaned toward Samir until their faces were almost touching, so close he could smell Samir's sweat. "You have to believe me. If *you* don't believe me, who will?"

"I don't know." Samir's voice sounded a little less judgmental. "But I know I won't be able to believe it unless I see it. Are you going to show me?"

Charlie thought about it for a moment. "Okay. I'll try to show you. It might not work, though. It might only work with me. But I can't show you tonight. I'll try tomorrow night, but tonight I'm going to be busy."

Samir nodded.

Charlie could see it was an effort.

"I can wait that long," Samir said.

Charlie pushed his bike through the loose gravel, back onto the pavement. He shifted the bag on his rack and started to pedal. He kept on, straight south on 232nd Street, and all the way to Zero Avenue, where he had to make a decision, right or left. The road didn't go any further.

Straight in front of them, the towering forest stretched east and west, as far as the eye could see. Somewhere, on the other side of that dark bank of trees, was the imaginary line that separated the two countries. And somewhere, in a small clearing, was the family he had watched under cover of night.

Charlie poked his fingers through the vents in the top of his helmet and scratched his head. Was it left or right? His instinct told him right, and not too far, probably not as far as the next main intersection. He scanned above the forest, checking for smoke, but there was nothing to see but blue sky.

Zero Avenue was empty. Even in broad daylight, it was hard to imagine an eerier stretch of road. Some derelict-looking farms, with rusted-out tractors and leaning sheds, stretched away to the north, but they all looked deserted. Otherwise, there was nothing but empty scrub and the moonscape rubble of old gravel pits.

Charlie glanced back at Samir and shrugged. "I think it's this way."

He pedalled slowly, his eyes trained on the forest to his left, searching for a spot he recognized.

It was like looking for a needle in a haystack—forest, obelisk, forest, obelisk. How would he know when he was close to the clearing where he'd seen the family?

And then he saw it, the white obelisk, just like all the others, except for the perfect Christmas tree standing right beside it. Charlie half-expected to see decorations dangling from the branches.

He shivered. Somewhere in there was the family. He hoped they were still okay. At least it wasn't raining. He shoulder-checked and coasted across the road.

Samir pulled up beside him. "Here?" His voice was heavy with doubt.

"Pretty sure." Charlie pulled his bike through the overgrown ditch, and bounced it over the low-growing brush. He leaned it up against the border marker, and motioned for Samir to do the same. He began to unstrap the stuffed green garbage bag.

Samir stood back, watching him. "Now what?"

"We hide these." Charlie started to drag his bundle toward the edge of the forest.

Samir shook his head and followed. "Why? Why don't we just take the stuff to the people?"

Charlie stopped and bit his lip. His plan was a little vague on details. "I don't want to scare them."

"We won't scare them. We'll just say hi and show them the stuff."

Charlie stared into the deep shade of the trees. Samir was trying to be helpful.

"And then," Samir continued, "if I saw them, maybe I'd start to believe about the flying."

Charlie let go of the bag and turned to face Samir. "I think they don't want to be found. They're way out here in the bush. If they wanted to be found, they wouldn't be here. I just want to help them, not blow their cover." He looked up at the sound of a passing truck. "And if you don't believe me about the flying, well then, you don't."

Samir started to walk in the direction they'd been going. "Don't get huffy."

Charlie swallowed. Samir was right. It was a lot to take in. He grasped the top of the bag and started to walk again.

"Okay." Samir was back to being normal. "So, then what? We stash the bags, and then how do they get the stuff?"

"I come back tonight with Buster. I move the bags closer, so they'll find them."

"But why? Why not tell the police?"

Charlie looked down at the bulging bag at his feet. "I probably will, but just not yet. Maybe they need a little time to sort things out, and this way, at least they won't starve or freeze to death." He couldn't get the pictures of Jayden and Tyler out of his head. People didn't have it easy. Things went wrong.

Samir narrowed his eyes. "They must be smuggling drugs. Why else would they be holed up at the border?" He waggled his finger at Charlie. "You should report them."

Charlie yanked a branch over the bags. How could Samir not get it? "They're not smuggling drugs," he said.

Chapter 28

PIZZA

Charlie was still mad at Samir when he got home. Not really mad. More like irritated. Samir had been a huge help, transporting the bags. But he was wrong about the smuggling. Charlie was sure of that.

He left his bike in the garage and headed around the back. The wind had come up, and it was suddenly cold. At least the grass wasn't growing so fast. That was one chore he wouldn't have to think about soon.

Buster was up on his hind legs, his front paws skittering along the top rail of the pen.

"Good old boy," Charlie said. He pulled up the bottom board so Buster could shimmy out.

Buster shook himself, slobber flying, and took off in a frenzy of zoomies.

Charlie sat down, and waited until Buster ran out of steam and collapsed, panting, on the grass beside him.

Buster stretched his head up and licked inside Charlie's ear. Then he flopped over, exposing his pink underbelly.

"Itchy tummy?" Charlie leaned over and scratched, noticing again all the white fur mixed in with the brown. "I told Samir about the flying," he said. "He didn't believe me. And he thinks the family is smuggling drugs."

Buster flipped over, so he was sitting on his haunches, eye to eye with Charlie. He made a harrumphing sound deep in his chest.

"I know," Charlie said. "I told him it was the dumbest thing I'd ever heard."

Buster laid his head on Charlie's shoulder.

Charlie could feel the dog's hot breath on his neck. "Anyway, the main thing is, we go back tonight. Put the stuff where they can find it, and then, what do you think? Try to get them some help?"

Buster licked Charlie's nose.

"Right," Charlie said. "I think so, too."

Buster stood up and gazed off in the direction of his food bowl.

"Okay," Charlie said. "I get it. Dinner."

◆

He was still choked at Samir as he trudged up the back stairs. The smell of pizza took him by surprise. He started to feel a little better.

Mom was bent over the open oven door, checking to see if the pizza was done.

Charlie peered over her shoulder. "Ham and pineapple?"

"Your favourite. Two more minutes," she said. "Can you call your brother and set the table?"

Mark must have smelled pizza, too. He was on the stairs before Charlie had a chance to open his mouth. He shot Charlie an elbow to the solar plexus as he cruised into the kitchen.

Mom pulled two pans out of the oven, and slid one of the pizzas onto a cutting board.

"This is nice," she said, handing the platter to Charlie. "Nobody has to rush out. No soccer practice. No work." She tapped her forehead with her pointing finger. "This calls for a celebration." She reached into the pantry cupboard, and pulled out the crooked beeswax candles Charlie had made in Grade 3. She'd been saving them. "Light these, will you?"

"Candles?" It wasn't Charlie's idea of a celebration.

"Don't be a jerk." Mark stepped in front of Charlie, and made a big show of lighting the candles. He waved the still-smoking match in Charlie's face. "It's not just about you."

"Like, you're so into candles," Charlie said, and made a bunch of slobbery smoochy sounds.

"Boys." Mom's voice cracked.

Charlie instantly felt bad. She was trying to make it special. He hit the dimmer switch—creating a little mood lighting. It was the least he could do. Then he headed downstairs, returning with a six-pack of pop from the storage room. He held up the cans. "Seeing as how we're celebrating?"

Mom sighed. "Fine."

The candlelight flickered as they settled into their chairs. Charlie's gaze fell on his dad's empty place, and his stomach twisted. He glanced at Mom. He stood up, almost toppling his own chair. He grabbed Dad's empty one, and shoved it into the alcove by the door.

Mom shook her head when he sat back down. "Was that necessary?"

And then, as if the mood was spoiled anyway, she pointed her knife at Charlie. "And another thing. I was going to make myself a slice of raisin toast this afternoon. I'd been thinking about it all morning. With that sharp cheddar I bought." She paused. "Any idea where those two things might be?"

Charlie's brain fogged. "Samir and I—I thought it was okay."

"But all of it?"

Mark leaned back on his chair and folded his arms across. "Like I said, Charlie. It's not just about you."

Mom glared at Mark.

And at that moment, a snuffling noise attracted their attention.

Charlie was at the kitchen door in two strides. He knew without looking, what he would see on the other side.

Buster sat, his head tilted, looking hopefully into the warmth and light of the kitchen. A long thread of drool dangled from one side of his mouth.

Mom stood up, banging her pizza slice onto her plate. "Charlie! How did that dog get out?"

Charlie caught Buster by the collar just as he was making a slinking dive for a spot under the table.

"Yeah, Charlie," Mark piped up. "How did that dog get out of the pen you built? Or maybe he just flew out?"

Charlie blanched. Had Samir told? He stared open-mouthed at his brother.

Mark shrugged and smirked.

"Did you even feed him? Does he have water? Isn't this just what I said would happen?" Mom pushed her chair back. "Charlie, it's just one thing after another. You've brought Buster home without checking with me. You take food without asking. And you, of all people," she took a deep breath, "you tell me you can look after a dog, and you can't make it happen, even for one weekend."

She spun on her heel and slammed out of the kitchen.

Charlie didn't have the energy to shout. "I did feed him," he whispered. "And I did give him water. And, I think his escape was just a little beyond my control." He didn't dare look at Mark. Hot tears filled his eyes.

Charlie sank back into his chair and considered the pizza on his plate. It was already starting to look cold and greasy. He let go of Buster's collar.

Buster sank down under the table and laid his head on Charlie's knees.

It was the first time Charlie noticed that Buster had eyelashes. He held the dog's head in both hands and scrubbed behind his ears.

Mark pushed the platter of pizza across the table. "Give him a slice. And then you better get him back in the pen."

Charlie nodded. He checked the slice for onions. The tears leaked out.

Mark reached across the table and gave him a noogie, a soft one, not the usual brain crusher. "You've got a lot goin' down right now," he said. "But she'll get over it. Don't worry."

◆

When Mom came into his room later that night, it was all Charlie could do to concentrate on what she was saying. He was miles away in his head, the wind in his hair, his body wrapped around Buster, the dense black forest stretched out below him in the dark. She sat on the side of his bed, frowning.

"Are you feeling okay? You looked really flushed at dinner, and now you're white as a sheet. Let me feel your forehead."

"I'm fine, Mom. You worry too much."

"I do worry too much. It's true." She looked around

at Charlie's room, as if she was trying to find the answer to a puzzle, somewhere in the posters on the wall, or the jumble of objects on the dresser.

"I'm sorry."

They said it at the same time, and all the tension melted out of the room.

Mom felt his forehead again. "Did you get any sleep at Samir's?"

"Yeah, we were up pretty late, I guess. I'm okay. Just tired."

"Well, get some sleep. Did you remember your dad is coming tomorrow?"

Charlie nodded. He had completely forgotten. He was supposed to have decided on something they would do together.

She hovered at the door. The wind had come up. They both listened to it buffeting the window.

Charlie's heart ached for Buster. He hoped he was warm enough. "Sorry about the raisin bread," Charlie said.

Mom smiled and raised her eyebrows. "And the oranges?"

"That, too."

She flicked off the light and pulled the door closed.

Chapter 29

WIND IN THE NIGHT

Charlie waited until his eyes were accustomed to the darkness before pulling out his flashlight.

First, he set his watch alarm for 1:30 in the morning. Then he put his clothes beside his bed, where he could find them fast. He'd left his shoes and jacket by the sliding door downstairs.

He pulled the duvet over his shoulders, and watched the moving pattern of branches that played back and forth on his bedroom wall. Through the open window, he could hear the trees pushing against each other in the wind. He sat up and looked out, to see if he could tell which way the wind was blowing.

Finally, Charlie dropped back down onto his pillow and closed his eyes. It seemed like sleep would never come.

And when it did, it was filled with images jumbled together in crazy sequences. Dogs drifting on logs in the river, howling to be rescued. Soccer players throwing rocks at the windows of the school. A fire in the garage and smoke everywhere.

When the alarm beeped, he breathed a sigh of relief, grateful to be delivered from his nightmares. He fumbled around under the pillow for his watch, and jammed his finger on the stop button. He held his breath. The house was silent.

His clothes felt clammy, and he shivered as he pulled them on over his pyjamas. He stuffed his extra pillow under the duvet, to make it look like he was where he was supposed to be. He opened the door a crack, listening again.

He crept downstairs, keeping to the side of the steps so they wouldn't creak. The kitchen still smelled like pizza. Charlie's mouth watered. He thought about grabbing a leftover slice from the fridge, but the fridge door always made a loud sucking noise when it closed. So, no pizza. Maybe for breakfast.

The tiles were cold on his bare feet, as he hesitated a moment, before heading into the basement. The clock on the stove marked the seconds with a soft click. But otherwise, the only sound was the wind shrieking loud in the kitchen, even with all the windows shut.

Buster was already up, his tail wagging, his nose pressed against the sliding door.

Charlie found his shoes and jacket, right where he'd left them. He pulled on the locking pin and slid the door open, just enough to fit through.

The wind hit him like a football tackle. "Whoa," he whispered. "Windy!" He pulled up the board to let Buster out, and crawled out after him.

Buster leaned against Charlie's knees, his ears flapping.

Charlie knelt down. "Do you think you can still fly in this? It's pretty wild."

Buster cocked his head, like he was thinking it over.

Charlie studied Buster's face. "It'd be good to get them the blankets and stuff, but I don't want to take any chances."

Buster opened his mouth and whined.

"What's that supposed to mean?" Charlie pulled his tuque down over his ears, thinking about what he'd said. It *was* kind of funny, when he thought about it. Flying around in the dead of night on a Labrador Retriever—it went without saying, they were taking chances. He bent down, so he was eye to eye with Buster. "Well, can you or can't you?"

Buster pointed his nose toward the compost bin Then he shook himself and started to trot toward the bottom of the yard.

A twig came spinning out of the trees and scudded across the patio. Buster had melted into an inky silhouette in the darkness.

"Okay. We're doing this." Charlie zipped his jacket right to the top and sprinted down the grass. As soon as he caught up with Buster, he lunged. And in the same moment, they were airborne.

They cleared the cedar fence between Charlie's place and the house next door. Buster's legs churned in a steady rhythm. Charlie hunkered down low, so they were more aerodynamic.

"Good boy, Buster," he said.

And that was the last thing he said, before they cleared the shelter of the trees at the bottom of the yard, and came into the full force of the wind.

The blast caught Buster broadside and seemed to pick them up and plunge them down.

Buster yelped.

It was a sound Charlie had never heard him make before. He clung to Buster's ruff, his head down on the dog's neck as they lurched like a leaf in the wind, pushed and tumbled and dropped.

Buster's legs thrummed powerfully, as he tried to maintain their course. Another sharp gust tossed them like a kite.

Buster yelped again, a strangled gasp of terror, before they tipped completely sideways.

The world turned upside down, and the blood rushed to Charlie's head. He screamed, barely conscious of the sky full of stars that swept across his vision.

Buster cranked his head around and pointed his nose toward the earth, so when the next gust caught them, he seemed to paddle back into an upright position. He kept his head up, and they flew higher and higher.

Charlie sobbed into Buster's rippling shoulder muscles. How stupid, stupid, stupid, he thought. To fly on Buster in such a wind. He should have known better.

And then he held his breath, as silence filled his ears. He raised his head and took a quick trembling glance. The earth was very far below, a miniature nighttime world he could barely make out. Buster had moved them into a place above the wind. The frantic churning of his legs slowed to the usual rhythm. Charlie felt his own breathing begin to settle. He loosened his grip a little, and willed himself to look down again.

He studied the lines of light far below them. There was 232nd Street. And the place where it crossed the Fraser Highway, and up ahead, the spot where the regular pattern of streetlights stopped, where the road intersected with Zero Avenue. They were on course.

"Good boy, Buster," Charlie whispered. He let go with one hand, carefully reaching up and scratching Buster under his chin. "Very amazing, incredible, epic, good boy."

Buster kept his nose pointed straight at the dark empty space, where the line of streetlights came to an end. His ears rippled back, their velvet fur just touching Charlie's cheek.

Charlie's stomach lurched, and he grabbed again at Buster's ruff. They were starting their descent. He gritted his teeth, knowing they would have to force their way back through the wind that howled beneath them.

He tightened his grip and closed his eyes.

The wind hit them like a sucker punch. For a terrifying second, Buster's legs stopped churning. They plummeted toward the ground. And then, a stream of solid air caught them from below, as if a parachute had snapped open and stopped their downward plunge.

Buster's body shuddered with the effort, as he pawed the air.

They tipped forward again. Buster was bringing them down in a sharp descent. The empty blackness of the forest materialized into menacing branches reaching out. A white obelisk glinted just below. The earth shot up with the force of a blast, and they were down.

Charlie rolled away, hitting his head on a big stone. For moments, the world spun in a dark, out-of-control kaleidoscope, before the rush of the wind in the branches above registered in his brain. The rough grass around them was bent double, and the howling in the trees obliterated all other sound.

Charlie looked across at Buster, who lay, sides heaving, an arm's length away. The white whiskers around his muzzle glistened.

"I'm sorry," Charlie whispered. "I'm so sorry. I shouldn't have let you fly tonight. I should have known better." He reached across the space between them, and rubbed away the spittle around Buster's mouth. His voice grew quieter still. "I know you're too old for this. I should have figured out how to do it myself."

Buster lifted his head. He eyed Charlie intently.

"What?" Charlie said.

Buster wrinkled his brow.

"Okay, so you're not too old. I didn't think you'd be touchy about your age."

Buster licked his right forepaw.

Charlie took another minute to catch his breath. He sniffed the air. He smelled wood smoke, but no glimmer of firelight penetrated the darkness of the forest. He pushed himself up so he was squatting on his haunches.

Buster heaved himself up and shook.

"So," Charlie said. "If you're ready, we can move the bags." He stood up, leaning into the wind, and placed his hand on top of Buster's head. "Follow me."

But Buster sat.

Charlie knelt down and whispered right into Buster's ear. "The idea is, we move the bags from where Samir and I hid them, and we take them just to the edge of the clearing. If they're in their tent, which would be best, they won't see us, but they'll find the bags in the morning."

Buster raised a paw and placed it firmly on Charlie's chest.

"I know," Charlie said, taking the paw. "It's just to help them for now. Just to give them a little time. Then we'll get them real help." Charlie stood and bent his body into the wind. He could just make out the dark shape of the bags he and Samir had hidden.

And then he saw something else, not ten feet away from the bags, on the other side of a bush. He pulled his flashlight from his pocket.

It didn't make sense.

Cardboard boxes. Maybe a dozen. All the same.

He crept closer, so he could clearly see the printing on the side of the boxes. He recognized the logo.

Computers? Boxes of them. Brand new. Never opened. Stacked two deep.

And then the world burst apart.

Chapter 30

THE SLASH

Two men stepped out from behind the pile of boxes, one from either side, moving toward him in giant strides.

Charlie hardly recognized the sound of his own voice—a high-pitched shout that disappeared into the wailing of the wind. He wanted to back away, but he was frozen to the spot.

The men stopped, inches in front of him, one, a giant of a man, wearing a bulky jacket like Charlie's uncle wore for hunting. The other man was small, shorter even than Mom, a dark-coloured hoodie pulled up and shadowing half his face.

"What the ..." the small man snarled.

Charlie's paralysis flooded away. He turned to run.

But the big man was fast, grabbing the back of his jacket, and pulling him in so close that Charlie felt a horrible spray from his mouth when he spoke. "What are you doing here?" He spat the words.

Charlie fumbled to say something that would save him. "I'm ... walking my dog."

Both men's heads swivelled.

"I don't see a dog," the small man said.

And it was true. Charlie scanned the darkness for a glimpse of Buster. But there was no sign of him. Where was Buster?

"I *was* walking my dog. Earlier. But he went chasing after a rabbit, and now he's gone, and I'm looking for him." Charlie's heart hammered in his throat as the lies formed on his lips. "And now I'm waiting for my dad. He's coming to help me." The familiar ache twisted in Charlie's gut. Dad wasn't coming. Not now.

The two men looked at each other, and Charlie sensed the silent communication between them.

The big man tightened his grip. "Tie him up and let's get out of here."

"Not a chance," the small man snorted. "He's had too good a look at us." He swung his head around, in the direction from which they'd come. "I say we take him back with us, on a little road trip, and let our friend decide what to do with him."

The big man sucked on his top lip, and then gave Charlie a shove. "How about a nice trip to America?" He laughed, an ugly, sneering bray, and pushed Charlie ahead of him.

"But my dad!" Charlie gasped.

The little man laughed. "Your dad," he sneered. "He's just going to have to look for your dog all by himself." He said it like he knew for sure there was no dog, and no dad coming.

Charlie stumbled and tripped ahead of the big man. Past the pile of boxes. Past the path he would have taken, into the clearing where the family was living. He was heading south. Heading for Washington.

The man kept a vice grip on Charlie's jacket, steering him with brute force. Stepping to the right. Moving ahead. Stepping to the left. And Charlie knew in a flash they were avoiding cameras and sensors. The man knew, just as Samir's dad had said, how to cross between Canada and the United States, and stay away from the sensors that would alert the border police. The computers were being smuggled in. The men knew what they were doing, but they hadn't counted on running into a kid in the dead of night.

Charlie shivered uncontrollably, trapped in the burly man's grip.

They snaked their way through the trees, stopping when they reached an empty, open space, that seemed to stretch forever into the black night. *The slash.* Samir's dad had described it well.

But how would they cross it? They would surely be spotted, with no trees for cover. He stood, face into the wind, panting, the big man's iron grip on the back of his jacket.

The small man pulled a phone out of his pocket and held it ahead of him. Charlie and his captor fell into step directly behind him.

They were crossing the slash according to an exact route, spelled out on the man's phone. They moved quickly, obviously not for the first time, and they had total darkness on their side. Charlie looked for the moon, but it had set, and its ghostly light was no help now. The men had figured out everything ahead of time, all except for meeting up with him.

On the other side of the slash, they pushed their way through brush that caught at Charlie's face. He was desperate to escape, but it took all his concentration to keep from tripping, and bringing the big man down on top of him.

Ahead of them, the other man stopped, pulling a fistful of keys from his pocket.

Charlie shuddered as he realized what he was looking at. The dense blackness straight ahead was the yawning, open back of a cube truck, empty now, its cargo of computers already handed off to Canada. He thought of the stash of boxes he'd stumbled upon. No wonder the men knew the route well. It would have taken them many trips to carry them all to the drop-off spot.

"Here's your ride," the big man grunted.

Charlie panicked. Where was Buster? If there was ever a time he needed a flying dog, it was right now. "Buster!" he shouted into the wind.

The man pushed Charlie to the truck's open back.

Charlie braced himself with one hand against the unyielding steel of the door frame. And at the cold touch of the metal, an idea shimmered briefly in the frenzy in his brain. He slid his other hand up to the top of his zipper, grasped it and began to inch it down.

"They'll find my phone," he said. His voice echoed in the truck's black open space.

"What phone is that?" the man in the hoodie said, his voice dripping with sarcasm.

"The one I took your pictures with, while I was watching you move the boxes," Charlie said evenly, as he felt the clasp at the bottom of the zipper give way.

He waited.

The small man moved in, so he was practically speaking into Charlie's ear, the sour smell of cigarettes filling Charlie's nose. "Where is this so-called phone?"

"On a stump. Where I put it. My dog will find it. My dad will see it. And you'll end up behind bars." Charlie shook with terror, wondering where he found the courage even to speak.

"He's lying." The man jangled his keys and stepped away from Charlie.

The big man tightened his grip on Charlie's jacket, so Charlie was practically lifted off his feet. "I don't know," he said. "Pictures would be bad."

"There's no phone," the other man said. "He's bluffing."

The big man shifted his weight, turning to face his partner. "Kids always have phones these days."

Charlie felt the tension on the jacket slacken. This was the moment. It was now or never.

He dropped to his knees, lifting his arms straight out behind him, and sliding out of the jacket, which was still in the big man's grip.

The two men shouted in unison.

But Charlie had made his escape!

Chapter 31

ESCAPE

Charlie crawled forward underneath the truck, shimmying over dirt and stones and bits of broken glass, until his fingers touched the knobby surface of the right front tire. He could tell from their grunting and shuffling, that the men were down on their hands and knees at the back of the truck, trying to see him in the inky darkness.

He waited for one frantic second for them to stand up, then plunged out from under the truck, and ran headlong into the cover of the surrounding bush. He fought his way through tree branches, tripping on roots, and sliding in the muck of the forest floor.

Mr. Grewal's words spun round in his brain. The sensors. The spies. The cameras. If he could make it back to the slash, he had a chance.

He pushed on, branches scraping his face and brambles catching at his jeans, until finally, he burst through the trees into the open space that marked the actual border between the two countries. He threw himself forward, running here and running there, back and forth, leaping into the air, trying to make himself as big and noticeable as possible. If the men had known the exact route to follow to avoid the sensors, Charlie did the opposite, trying every way he could to trigger an alarm and alert the border patrol.

From the forest behind him, the men's shouts rang out, but he didn't dare look back. He ran and dodged, and zigzagged back and forth, in the dark open space of the slash. The seconds stretched into agonizing minutes. Then, just when he thought his lungs would burst, a faraway sound reached him.

The whoop-whoop-whoop of a helicopter pushed its way into Charlie's brain. He stopped and listened, sweat pouring down his face.

And then there were lights, penetrating beams from all sides, and the sweep of a helicopter searchlight.

Charlie put his hand up to shield his eyes from the blinding light, and started to laugh uncontrollably. He leapt into the air and then sprinted toward the lights, waving his arms.

"I'm here! I'm here!" he shouted.

Silhouetted forms materialized in the darkness. Beams from flashlights crisscrossed over the rough-mown open space. Charlie ran as fast as his shaking legs could carry him, straight into the arms of a uniformed officer, who fumbled her flashlight as his body collided with hers.

Charlie's hysterical laughter dissolved into wrenching sobs.

The officer caught Charlie by the shoulders and held him at arm's length, as five of her colleagues closed in around them.

The deafening throb of the helicopter began to lessen as it moved off a little. And after a second or two, Charlie heard a jumble of voices and radio static coming from a nearby patrol car.

The police officer loosened her hold.

Charlie stepped back a little, looking first into the policewoman's wide-open eyes, and then at the others. He was shivering so hard he could barely speak, but he forced the words out. "Thank you," he said. "I didn't know you'd come so fast."

The female officer took the lead.

"We're going to want to know your name and where you live, and then we'll want the rest of the story. But let's get you into the squad car first. We'll get you warmed up."

The other officers made a move to disperse.

Charlie shook his head firmly. "No. Wait. You have to get the bad guys first."

The group froze. Six sets of eyes bore into Charlie's.

"Yes," the female officer prompted. "Definitely, tell us about the bad guys first."

Charlie pointed in the direction from which he'd run. "Their truck is there, maybe half a kilometre back. They're smuggling computers into Canada."

"How many guys?" an officer asked.

"Two. A big one wearing a bulky coat, and a smaller guy wearing a hoodie. They stink like cigarettes."

"Oh, man, don't you hate that?" another officer grinned.

But the rest were all seriousness, listening intently, hands reaching for their guns. The thrum of the helicopter was back.

Chapter 32

SHAUNIE AND ORAM

"What kind of truck?" "How many minutes ago?" the officers wanted to know.

Charlie answered all their questions the best he could, then watched as four of them raced away, leaving him with the female officer and her partner. She motioned for him to follow, and he fell into step behind them, working hard to keep up.

When they got to the patrol car, she opened the back door and reached under the seat. "Here," she said, handing him a blanket sealed in a plastic pouch, the kind they give out on airplanes. "In you get," she said.

He'd never been in the back of a police car before. Wait till he told Samir. There was no upholstery on the seat, just hard plastic, and no handles on the doors.

"Cool," Charlie said, sliding into the brightly lit space.

The officers got into the front seat and slid back the

plexiglass partition. The dash looked like the cockpit of an airplane.

The male officer got on the radio immediately.

The female officer started the engine and then turned to face Charlie. "We'll have you warmed up in no time." She pointed to the keyboard in front of the other officer. "So, let's have it. Right from the beginning. What's your name, and what the Sam Hill are you doing out here in the middle of the night, trying to get the attention of the border patrol?" Her smile lit up the car.

Charlie thought fast. Where to begin? One thing was sure. He wasn't going to tell them about Buster, at least, not about the flying.

His stomach twisted at the thought of Buster. Where *was* he? Charlie's heart ached at the thought that something awful had happened to him. It wasn't like Buster to disappear at the moment of crisis. But where was he?

The easy part was telling his name and where he lived. Then it got hard. There was so much he couldn't share. Like the fact that he'd flown there on his dog. They'd never believe him. His throat started to pinch as he tried to speak.

"So," he paused, trying out a few starters in his

head. "A couple of days ago, I was here with my dog, Buster. Well, actually, it's not my dog. I volunteer at Dr. Anderton's, and Buster is living there right now, while Dr. Anderton tries to find him a home. Anyway, we found this family, a mom and dad and a baby."

The female officer interrupted him. "I'm Shaunie by the way," she said. "And this is my partner, Oram. Okay, so you found this family?"

"Right. They're living right near here. In a tent. They look really poor and sad, like they have no friends and no one to help them. And the man is limping. A lot. So, he can't get stuff for them, like he thought he'd be able to."

Shaunie interrupted him. "When you say, 'near here,' where exactly are you talking about?"

Charlie tried to look outside to get his bearings, but the glass all around reflected only a broken-up image of his own face peering out.

"They're on the Canadian side, in the forest, where there's a bit of a clearing, and they're between 232nd and 224th."

Oram hammered away at his keyboard, looking up whenever Charlie paused.

"But they're not bad people," Charlie said. "I don't

want them to get in trouble. They're just trying to live."

Shaunie stopped writing and studied Charlie. "So, what did you do, once you'd found them?"

"I was going to try to get help for them, but first I wanted to give them some food and blankets, so they wouldn't be cold and hungry. I thought they might just need a little time, for the guy's foot to get better, and to figure out a plan." He thought for a second. "And also, I wanted them to know that somebody cared about them."

She chewed the end of her pen. "So, tonight?"

"I was bringing them blankets and stuff, and that's when I saw the boxes of computers. And right then, the two guys grabbed me."

Oram, who didn't look much older than Mark, glanced back at Charlie. "You've had quite the scary time," he said. "But I don't get why it's all going down in the middle of the night."

"I know," Charlie said. "When I think about it now, it seems dumb, but I didn't want them to see me and think I'd blow their cover. I was going to sneak the stuff in, so they'd see it in the morning and be happy."

The two officers gave each other a look, like maybe they'd captured a space alien.

Charlie squirmed.

Then a thought occurred to him. He pointed to the computer on the dash. "So, have you already told on them?"

Shaunie stifled a laugh. "I wouldn't say, *told on*. We've reported their whereabouts to the Aldergrove detachment of the RCMP. That's all."

"But what will happen to them now?" Charlie's heart sank at the thought of police and dogs descending on the family. They'd be terrified already, with the helicopter overhead, and all the lights and noise. They'd be wondering what was happening in their already scary world.

Shaunie shifted a little, so she was looking right into Charlie's eyes. "You know, Charlie, everything happens for a reason. We're supposed to get torrential rain tomorrow. They'd be soaked and frozen if they had to face that. It's better this way. Family Services will kick in. With any luck, they'll be in warm beds, with food in their stomachs, before the rain hits."

"I just thought they needed a little time."

Shaunie faced forward and put the car in gear, still locking eyes with Charlie in the rear-view mirror. "They don't *have* to leave. If they really want to stay, no one is going to force them to leave. They haven't done anything wrong."

The car started to move over the rough ground. Shaunie glanced at Oram, and then back at Charlie. "Well," she said, "shall we take you home?"

Charlie flopped back on the cold vinyl seat. What a mess he'd made. He'd practically got himself abducted by smugglers. Buster was missing. He was being escorted home in the middle of the night in a border patrol car. He'd spoiled everything for the family in the forest. Mom was going to kill him. And Dr. Anderton would give him a stern look that said, *I knew I shouldn't have said yes to you about volunteering at the clinic, and now you've lost Buster.*

He twisted around and tried to look out the back window, desperately hoping to catch a glimpse of the flying brown Labrador with the giant heart. But all he could see was his own worried face looking back at him.

Chapter 33

THE PRODIGAL SON

Charlie pulled the blanket up around his shoulders, watching the streetlights click by, barely conscious of the radio chatter coming from the computer on the dash.

That is, until he heard his name, loud and clear, coming through the static.

He sat bolt upright, holding his breath to see if he heard it again.

Oram glanced up from the keyboard and grinned. "Sounds like there's a party at your place," he said. "Your parents must have figured out you were missing and called the police. There's a squad car at your house now."

Charlie gasped and sank back in his seat, his head in his hands. All hell was breaking loose in his life. Mom would be freaking. Buster was missing. His gut wrenched as he thought about Buster. Where had he disappeared to? Was he caught in a trap? Where was he?

"Do they know I'm with you?" he asked.

"They do now," Oram said, finishing a keyboard stroke with a flourish. "The prodigal son is on his way home."

Charlie wasn't sure what prodigal meant, but he had a feeling it had something to do with being unbelievably stupid and irresponsible. Letting the blanket slip down, he watched as the familiar blocks slid past.

He gulped when they turned down his street. Every light in his house and Samir's house was on. Charlie's front door was wide open, with people crowding around it. A police car was backing out of the driveway.

The two cars pulled up beside each other and both drivers opened their windows.

"The eagle has landed," Shaunie said to the driver of the other vehicle.

He stretched his head around so he could get a look at Charlie, acknowledging him with a two-finger salute.

Charlie smiled weakly, giving him a pathetic wave.

Shaunie rolled up her window and pulled into the driveway. "Home again, home again," she said getting out and opening Charlie's door.

Charlie was trying to fold up the blanket, when a volley of excited barks split the air.

Buster!

Charlie leapt from the car and flew across the grass, at the same speed Buster was racing out to meet him. They collided in a frenzy of dog and boy and slobbery kisses. Buster emerged on top, forepaws planted on Charlie's chest, tail waving in wild circles of joy.

Charlie lay back, his eyes on the beautiful brown Labrador. Buster was alive. He was here. By some totally awesome, unbelievable miracle, Buster was okay. Charlie closed his eyes to keep back tears of relief, savouring the moment, before he had to face everyone.

He opened his eyes. Dad was here! Mom. Mark. Samir. Samir's mom and dad. Buster. And in the second row, hanging back and grinning, Oram and Shaunie.

Dad reached down a hand.

Charlie took it and clambered to his feet, feeling much safer now, with his hand in Dad's much bigger one.

Dad brushed the grass off Charlie's back and held him out at arm's length. "You're okay." It was a statement, not a question.

Charlie could see the relief in Dad's face.

"You've caused quite the uproar. Your mom's been sick with worry."

Before he could respond, Samir's mom reached in and squeezed his shoulder. "I'm glad you're home safe, Charlie," she said. Then she motioned to her husband and Samir that it was time for them to go.

Charlie tried to catch Samir's eye, but Samir seemed mesmerized by the glowing cockpit of the border patrol car. He was still staring at it when his mom gave him a sharp tug.

Charlie drilled his gaze into Samir's retreating back, willing him to turn around. They had to talk.

And Samir got the message. He pulled free of his mom's grip and darted back to Charlie.

"I'm glad you got home safe," he said, so everyone could hear. But he mouthed the next words soundlessly. "I didn't tell about the flying."

Charlie could have hugged him.

Samir jogged back toward his parents, and Charlie watched, as they filed into their own house and the lights started to blink off.

Then it was Mark and Mom and Dad speaking, all at once, until Dad said, "We need to go inside and let this neighbourhood get back to sleep." He motioned for Shaunie and Oram to go ahead of them.

Mark hung back with Charlie. "Dude," he said, and Charlie knew what he meant.

Mark leaned down and grasped Buster's collar. "I'll put him in his pen, but don't start talking till I get there."

Inside the brightly lit kitchen, Charlie sank onto a stool at the island. The others stood around him. Charlie felt like a guppy in a fishbowl.

Mom's voice was quivery. "Thank you," she said to Shaunie and Oram. "He gave us quite a fright. It's not like him to disappear in the night and not tell anyone, not even his best friend. And Charlie," she folded her arms across her chest, "I think you owe these officers and the rest of us an apology."

But she didn't give him time to say anything. She dropped onto a stool like her legs had given out. "What kind of irresponsible, harebrained thing were you up to, anyway?"

That's when Dad seemed to notice the badges on the officers' uniforms.

"Border Security?" He scratched his head, and looked from the officers to Charlie and back again.

Shaunie moved over and put her arm around Charlie's shoulders. "Maybe I could give just a little background, before my partner and I head out." She looked down at Charlie. "Of course, it's always best to keep your parents informed as to your whereabouts," she said.

Then she spoke to his parents. "It's not often that we get a call to help out a kid, who's been able to successfully direct us to a smuggling operation we've been trying to close in on for months. But that's what happened this time."

Mark made a sputtering sound, like he was choking back a laugh.

Mom and Dad stared at Charlie.

"But even more unusual for us," Shaunie continued, "is to meet a young person, Charlie here, who puts his own safety and comfort at risk, to help someone less fortunate than himself. Charlie was out there tonight, taking food and blankets to a homeless family camping in the bush and running out of luck." She faced Charlie again. "The world would certainly be a better place if all our young people made the same effort."

Oram nodded his head and pointed his two index fingers in Charlie's direction.

Mom and Dad shifted their gaze to Shaunie, then back to Charlie.

"So, we're gonna get out of here and let you guys get some sleep," Shaunie said. She and Oram shook everyone's hand, before going with Dad to the front door.

Charlie followed.

At the door, Shaunie turned back and looked at Charlie. She put one hand up to shield her face from the others, and winked, and gave him an enthusiastic thumbs up with the other.

She pulled the door closed behind her with a firm thunk.

Chapter 34

IF IT HADN'T BEEN FOR BUSTER

After the patrol car pulled out of the driveway, silence filled the hallway. Mom, Dad, Mark, and Charlie stood frozen, looking at one another.

Mark broke the spell. "Dude," he said. "You totally scared us."

They all followed Mark into the kitchen, and watched him pull a box of cornflakes out of the cupboard and begin to fill up a bowl.

"Mark, it's four in the morning," Mom said.

Mark shrugged.

Mom sat at the table and leaned her chin into her hands. "I hardly know what to say." Tears filled her eyes and threatened to spill over.

Charlie swallowed.

She blew her nose noisily and smiled through her tears. "I'm just so grateful you're home, safe and sound."

Dad put his arm around Charlie's shoulders. "You have no idea what we all went through here. It was so unlike you to be gone in the night. And then, when Samir didn't know where you were—we couldn't figure out what was going on."

Charlie kept his eyes on the floor. Something didn't add up. Samir had kept his mouth shut. How would they have known he wasn't in his bed?

Mom filled in the blanks. "If it hadn't been for Buster, we'd have had no idea you were even gone."

Buster? Charlie looked at Mark for a clue. What did Buster have to do with it?

"Where is he, anyway?" Mom said.

"In his pen," Mark mumbled, through a mouthful of cornflakes.

Mom squinted and tapped her fingertips on her lips. "Maybe he should come inside. Just this once."

Charlie held his breath.

"Mark?" Dad cocked his head toward the stairs.

"Going," Mark said.

"That dog," Mom sighed. "He put up the biggest ruckus you've ever heard. Somehow, he'd got out of his pen, and he was at the front door, barking like a mad thing.

Then, when I opened the door, he blew past me like I was invisible, and bolted up to your room, barking so loud, I thought he'd wake the whole neighbourhood."

Buster slipped into the kitchen, and settled himself inconspicuously under the table.

Mom reached down to scratch behind his ears.

"Mom!" Charlie couldn't believe his eyes. "Your allergies!"

"I know. I'm being very careful not to put my hands near my face, and I'll wash them very thoroughly."

She looked around. Three sets of disbelieving eyes were trained on her.

"I know. It's just that—you know—he's homeless at the moment. And if it hadn't been for Buster, we'd never have known ..." She stopped mid-sentence, staring at Charlie, like she'd just remembered something. "Where were you? And what were you thinking of, going off by yourself like that in the middle of the night? And what's all this about homeless people?"

Charlie braced himself. Where to start? Which parts to tell? Which parts to leave out? He turned his head and caught Mark's eye. Mark would laugh himself sick, and tell all his friends about Charlie's over-active imagination, if Charlie even so much as raised the possibility of flying around on a dog. He opened his mouth to speak, still having no idea what words would come out.

Dad spoke first. "I need to get home. It's almost morning. What if we leave the full disclosure until tomorrow? I want to hear the whole story, but for now, Charlie is home safe, and that's all that matters. Let's do this after lunch tomorrow." He stood up and faced Charlie. "I want to hear every gory detail, and then I think we need to re-establish some basic rules for staying out of trouble."

Dad wanted to go *home*, a place that wasn't here. It shocked Charlie that Dad could describe the new reality so easily. But it bought him time.

"Great idea." He faked a yawn. "I'm exhausted."

Mom looked doubtful. "All right." She stood up. "Better put Buster back in his pen."

Buster's nails clicked on the tile floor as he scrabbled stiffly to his feet. He leaned his full weight against Charlie's legs.

Charlie scratched under Buster's chin.

Mom put her arms around Charlie and gave him a quick peck on his cheek. "See this grey?" she said, pulling the hair at the top of her head. "I'm pretty sure it wasn't there when I got up this morning. Mark, don't forget to turn out the light."

◆

Curled up in his warm duvet, Charlie lived it all over again. The turbulent flight, especially the part where the strongest gust pushed them upside down. The shock of seeing the boxes of computers piled up. And then, without any warning, the two men coming at him. His pulse raced as he relived the way the big man had pushed him, and the awful, black, echoing interior of the cube truck. What if he hadn't escaped? What if they'd shoved him in there? He shuddered at the thought. And Samir's dad had been totally right about the border. A wave of relief washed over Charlie as he recalled the whump-whump of the helicopter, just before the border police came running at him, the beams from their flashlights crisscrossing through the night.

And how strange it was that Buster had disappeared, right when Charlie needed him most. Almost like he knew he was no match for really bad guys, who probably had guns. And then he'd shown up here, to alert everybody that Charlie was gone.

And Dad. Charlie waited for the angry feeling to sweep across him. He waited some more, stomach tight, for the stab he felt, every time he thought about living his life without Dad. It didn't come. He waited some more.

But then, he thought, maybe it wasn't life without Dad. He'd been here tonight. He was coming tomorrow. He would "read the riot act." Charlie wasn't sure what "the riot act" was. It was what Mom always said Dad would do if Charlie was acting like a jerk, but it usually meant there'd be some yelling.

Charlie yawned, a real one this time. It was all starting to feel like a movie he'd watched a long time ago, and he couldn't quite remember how all the scenes fitted together.

But there was one part he remembered very clearly—Mom letting Buster come into the kitchen. Charlie turned over and pulled the covers up around his ears. She was softening. It was only a matter of time now.

Chapter 35

THREE CALLS

The shrill ring of the house phone jolted Charlie awake. He glanced at his clock—11:20 AM! He threw the duvet back.

What was going on? Mom never let him sleep this late. Buster would be dying to be let into the yard for a pee. Charlie pulled on a hoodie and yesterday's socks that were still rolled up beside his bed. He glanced outside. Rain was coming down, practically sideways, battering the window.

He headed for the bathroom, leaving the door open a crack to see if he could figure out who Mom was talking to on the phone.

Mom still had the phone tucked under her ear, and was writing something on the notepad, when Charlie padded downstairs into the kitchen.

She turned to look at him, making "uh-huh" sounds

into the receiver. When she set the phone down, she studied Charlie.

"We need to talk," she said.

He didn't want to have to tell the whole story twice. "Can't we do it later, when Dad's here? I have to let Buster out and feed him."

"Done. Your brother took pity on you."

"Still. We should wait, and I have to go see Buster."

"And we *can* wait, but I just need to tell you who's been phoning."

Charlie sat down. He was curious.

"First," Mom looked at her notes, "a Mrs. Wu from Social Services is going to call back again. She's the—" she squinted at her notes "—in-take person for social housing and community building. She wants to talk to you about the family you were supporting. Apparently, they want to thank you, and let you know they're going to be okay. They've been brought into temporary shelter, until there is something more long-term for them."

Charlie grinned, conscious of the rain still drumming against the windows. As Shaunie had predicted, it wasn't a morning to be shivering in a tent, with no food for your baby.

Mom was beaming. "She's going to call back. She wants to tell you personally. I'm really proud of you, Charlie. Sounds like you've done a wonderful thing for this family."

Charlie studied his toes, embarrassed by the attention, but bursting with pride at the same time.

But then Mom came over and stood right in front of him. She placed her hands on his shoulders.

A stillness settled over the house.

Mom cleared her throat. "And Dr. Anderton phoned."

Charlie's heart stopped. This wasn't how good news started. His voice came out as a squeak. "What did he say?"

"Oh, Charlie. I'm so sorry."

Mom's grip on his shoulders was so tight it almost hurt.

"He wanted to know how Buster had been over the weekend. I told him how much he loved it here, and what a good dog he was, and how well everything's been going." She put her hand up to her mouth. "And then he told me how the couple that had come to see about adopting him, called him at home, and they've made a firm decision to take him."

Charlie's legs buckled and he dropped onto the stool. "But did you tell him—?"

Mom didn't give him time to finish. "I did. I told him you'd been so responsible, and that Buster was happy here. But it turns out, the couple are close friends of his, and he originally promised them the dog ..."

Charlie felt like he'd been stabbed in the chest. "But you were going to let me keep him. I know you were going to let me keep him, Mom!"

"It's true. I was."

Mom put her arm around Charlie's shoulders. "And the worst of it is ..." she paused, as if she hated to say the next words, "they want to pick him up first thing tomorrow morning. Dr. Anderton would like us to bring him into the clinic later today."

"Not today." Charlie stormed downstairs and out the sliding door. It wasn't fair. Buster was his. They were a team. They had work to do. He threw himself down on Buster's bedding and wrapped his arms around his dog. Buster was the best thing that had happened to him since Dad .... A sob caught in his throat, and he couldn't stop the tears.

Buster panted in Charlie's ear, the velvet of his

muzzle against Charlie's cheek. Drips of warm saliva dribbled onto Charlie's neck.

"It's not fair," Charlie whispered. "We were just getting started."

Buster wiggled out of Charlie's grip and shook himself. Then he stretched forward on his front paws, his rump up in the air. "Stick," his eyes said, and he leapt up and pounded his front paws on the top rail of the pen.

Charlie choked back a sob, swiping at his eyes with the sleeve of his hoodie. "All right. Stick," he said, swinging the bottom board up and scrambling through, ahead of Buster.

Charlie ran headlong into the rain in his socks. The wind had strewn the yard with branches. He found a good one and threw it high.

Buster raced to retrieve it, caught it in his mouth, and the chase was on. Buster dodged and weaved. Charlie lunged and grabbed, skidding in the wet grass. His boxers and hoodie were soon soaked through. And Buster's coat streamed with water.

"Charlie!"

Charlie slid to a stop and looked up. Mom was

standing at the kitchen door, shielding her hair from the rain with a tea towel.

"I forgot to tell you. Shaunie phoned. They found your bike. She said they never would have spotted it in the dark, if it hadn't been for your blinking taillight. We can pick it up later today, when we take Buster to the vet's."

Chapter 36

VERTIGO

They'd found his bike?

Charlie crouched with the slobber-covered stick in his hand, the rain sluicing down his face.

Buster sat on his haunches, staring at the stick.

Charlie had heard about vertigo, when something in your ears makes you lose your balance, and you feel as if the world is spinning around you. Maybe that's what he had. His world was definitely spinning. He put his hand on Buster's head, trying to get his balance.

"They found my bike," he said.

Buster locked eyes with Charlie.

"Do you know anything about that?"

Buster's tail thumped. He covered Charlie's face with kisses, and finished by licking out his ear.

Charlie ran his hands over the thick wet fur of Buster's shoulders. He felt along the muscles of his legs, turning over his paws, and studying the rough pads of the soles of his feet.

He studied where the dog's legs joined his body, looking for some sign—a smudge of grease or a fleck of metallic blue paint—any evidence at all that Buster had somehow got his bike to the border.

Buster sighed, eyeing the stick lying in the grass.

Charlie held Buster's head in both hands. "I'm serious," he said. "How did my bike get down there?"

Buster tried to look away, but Charlie held his face gently in his hands, and looked deep into Buster's eyes.

"It didn't ride itself there," Charlie whispered. "Tell me the truth. Did you somehow fly it there?"

Buster thumped his tail twice, and then he lunged for the stick.

"Leave it," Charlie said, standing up. "I want to make sure I've got this straight. So, when the bad guys had me, you flew home, and barked and woke up Mom, so she'd call the police. Then later, when everyone was sleeping, you somehow got my bike down to Zero Avenue, so it would make sense to everyone how I got down there. Then you flew back here, and put yourself into your pen. And now, you're just an ordinary Labrador Retriever."

Buster sat back down on his haunches and stared off into space.

"Did you just say, *Duh*?" Charlie said.

Buster thumped.

"That's what I thought you said."

Buster stood up and shook.

Charlie watched him as he trotted down to the bottom of the yard, where the ravine began, and lifted a leg.

"Hey!"

It was Samir, at the front of the house, wearing his dad's rain poncho.

"Hey, Samir!" Charlie started up the grassy slope, hoping Samir hadn't overheard him talking to Buster.

"What're you doing out in the rain in your boxers?" He held out a samosa. "I would have eaten both, but Mom made me promise to save you one."

Charlie broke off a piece and gave it to Buster, who had hurtled to the front yard at the sight of Samir and the samosa.

"I don't get to keep Buster," Charlie said.

"Oh, dude," Samir said. "That's brutal."

Charlie waited for the question he knew was coming.

"So, did you end up having to tell your mom?"

"About what?" Charlie stalled.

"About Buster." Samir wasn't going to be the first to say it.

"What about him?" Charlie hedged.

"What you told me. About the flying."

Charlie reached down for the stick Buster had laid at his feet, and threw it toward the trees. His stomach felt tight. The last thing he wanted to do was *not* tell Samir the truth, but if he didn't get to keep Buster, then it was probably better to forget the whole flying dog story, before everyone at school heard it and thought he was crackers.

He looked up sheepishly. "I was only joking about the flying," he said. "Just being dumb. Sorry. I was having fun, wishing I had a magic dog. You know, like all the times we used to wish for crazy stuff."

They watched as Buster lay at their feet, ripping the stick apart and spitting out the pieces.

"It's not like I believed you." Samir sounded disappointed. "I just thought maybe you'd lost it."

Charlie was silent for a moment. "I think I did lose it," he said finally. He leaned up against the wooden swing Dad had built, a million years ago. "I think this whole thing with my dad really got to me." He stuck the last of the samosa in his mouth.

It was Samir's turn to try and wrestle what was left of the stick out of Buster's jaws. "Yeah," he said. "It would have been cool, though."

"Yeah, it would have been totally cool," Charlie agreed, imagining a Labrador Retriever on a bike, sailing through the air, glistening silver in the light of a full moon.

Buster looked up. A car was pulling into the driveway.

Dad. Right when he'd said he'd be here.

Charlie watched him get out of the car and wave. He was glad to see him. He didn't feel overwhelmed or, as Samir had put it, like he was going to lose it.

"Your dad's here," Samir said.

"Yeah." Charlie wiped his fingers on his wet boxers. "I'll come over later when he's gone." He lowered his voice so only Samir would hear. "He's come to read me the *riot act* about my behaviour," he said, his fingers making air quotes around riot act. "I better go."

Charlie fist-bumped Samir. Then he splashed across the sodden lawn to the driveway, Buster two steps behind him, the drool-covered stick firmly clenched in his mouth.

Chapter 37

THE RIOT ACT

Charlie's Dad had taken cover in the garage. "Hey, bud. You're soaked!" he said. "Better get yourself some dry clothes, and then ..." he waggled a carry-case of donuts.

The riot act, Charlie thought. But how bad could it be if Dad had brought donuts?

"I'll be right there," he said. He wrestled the stick out of Buster's mouth. "No more stick. Time to get dried off."

Buster stared at the stick.

"And get a cookie," Charlie added, and took off around the house to Buster's pen.

By the time he'd changed into his sweats and trudged downstairs, Dad was sitting at the counter with a mug of coffee in his hand, a pad of paper and a pen in front of him. It was going to be one of Dad's famous lists. He'd already written in the numbers. Mom leaned against the counter, her hands around her own mug.

Charlie sat down across from Dad, eyeing the donuts.

Dad slid the box across to him.

Charlie lifted the lid. Half were chocolate-glazed with sprinkles. His favourite.

"Okay," Dad said quietly. "Start at the beginning."

Charlie watched as Mark slipped quietly into the kitchen and settled on a stool, but his thoughts were far away. He was thinking back to his very first day at the vet's. The same day Dr. Anderton had come to work and found Buster, patiently waiting on the steps of the clinic, with the family from Toronto. He would tell Mom and Dad everything. About how Dr. Anderton had put him in charge of caring for Buster, about the rescues, and the terrifying encounter with the smugglers.

But not about the flying. That had to be his secret. They would worry too much, and maybe even think he needed serious help.

He reached for a donut, his mouth already watering, and started to talk.

When he was done, Dad cleared his throat and picked up the pen. "So," he said. "That's a lot to take in. A lot goin' down, as your brother would say."

Charlie slipped another donut onto his plate, waiting

for the words he knew Dad was about to say.

"What we need," Dad said, "is a list." He began to write. Charlie rolled his eyes at the title—"Charlie's Rules to Live By"—and listened, while Dad read aloud as he wrote.

1. No more middle-of-the-night rescue missions. (*Well, duh,* Charlie thought. There definitely wouldn't be any of those.)

2. You have to be more RESPONSIBLE. (Dad wrote *responsible* the way he said it, like it was permanently in capital letters.)

3. Bike lights must be kept charged, in case you need to get home from somewhere in the dark. (Charlie was pretty sure that was cancelled out by rule number one, but he wasn't in a position to argue.)

4. Mom and Dad must be kept informed about where you are. (Something that was impossible without a cellphone, Charlie reminded him, and Dad actually agreed.)

Dad pushed the list across the counter to Charlie. "We just want you to be safe."

Charlie looked up from the cream-filled donut he'd

been seriously considering. That was it? The riot act wasn't half as bad as he'd thought it would be. Maybe because he couldn't keep Buster, Dad was treating him like he had an incurable disease and would be dying soon.

"I know," Charlie said.

Dad glanced at his watch and stood up. "Hug?" he said.

Mom stepped in. Charlie stepped in. Even Mark stepped in. And Dad put his arms around them all. The hug lasted and lasted.

As soon as Dad was out the door, Charlie raced downstairs to Buster's pen. Every minute counted now. There wasn't much time left before he and Mom had to take Buster to meet Dr. Anderton at the clinic.

Buster must have heard him coming. His nose was pressed against the glass, and his tail was making 360's. When Charlie pulled open the sliding door, Buster blew by Charlie, making a beeline for the stairs up to the kitchen. Charlie stood, stunned. Buster had never come inside through the sliding door. It was like he knew. Seconds mattered.

Then, before he could react, Mom was coming down the stairs with her yoga mat. Charlie held his breath.

The encounter was over in a micro-second. Buster

slipped by Mom like he owned the place, and Mom harrumphed and shifted her mat to one side, to let him by. She was definitely going soft.

Buster ignored all the tempting smells in the kitchen, leading them directly to Charlie's bedroom. Once inside, Charlie plunked down on his bed, while Buster did a quick sniffing tour, paying special attention to the laundry basket in the closet. Then, without a moment's hesitation, he hopped up beside Charlie, sat on his haunches, and lifted a paw to Charlie's cheek. Charlie held it there, feeling the rough leather of Buster's paw against his skin.

Charlie sensed it. Buster was telling him something.

"What?" he said.

Buster looked away toward the window.

"Are you thinking about the flying we did?" Charlie asked.

Buster began to pant, like he was suddenly hot.

"And about Jayden?" Charlie stroked Buster's back, running his fingers over the ridges of his backbone.

"And Tyler? And the man and the lady and the baby down by the border?"

Buster leaned his head against Charlie's chest.

"I know," Charlie whispered into Buster's ear. "There's a lot of people having a hard time."

Buster licked inside Charlie's nose and Charlie just let it happen. He thought about his dad, the way his dad had looked exhausted, but relieved and happy, at three o'clock on Sunday morning. The way he'd pulled into the driveway today, just like he'd said he would. And the chocolate glazed donuts with sprinkles. And the riot act.

"I know," he whispered again. "He loves me. I can see that now."

Buster lifted his paw once more to Charlie's cheek. Then he executed three circles, put his head down on Charlie's pillow and fell asleep.

Charlie curled up beside him. "Goodbye, Buster," he said. He stroked Buster's front paws, feeling the ragged edges of his toenails. He ran his hands over Buster's flank, and felt his chest moving up and down. He grasped the thick ruff at Buster's shoulders, and thought of the way he'd clung on for dear life, his legs wrapped tightly around Buster's middle.

Oh, Buster, Charlie thought. *We flew. All those times. We really flew.* He lifted his head and tried to memorize Buster's sleeping form, so he would never ever forget.

◆

"Charlie!"

He came to with a start.

"We should go," Mom called from the bottom of the stairs.

It was time. Buster was already sitting beside the bedroom door, looking alert and ready.

Chapter 38

WORK TO DO

After school on Monday, Charlie wheeled his bike out of the bike compound, and tried not to think about Buster. Handing the leash over to Dr. Anderton yesterday was the second hardest thing he'd ever done. He looked at his watch. The Bairds would have picked Buster up at the clinic before eight o'clock this morning. They would already have taken the ferry to the Island, and arrived at their farm in the Comox Valley. Buster would be trying to settle into his new family, and wondering what on earth had happened to Charlie.

He fastened his helmet and set off, trying to get excited about seeing Megan, and finding out what jobs he might get to do today. He blinked back tears, dreading the sight of Buster's empty kennel.

At the four-way stop at the bottom of Saddlehorn Hill, Charlie waited for a bright red sports car to make a screeching left turn in front of him, before shifting into his lowest gear and starting up. By the time he made it to the top, he was sweating like a pig. He pulled down the zip on his jacket and coasted down the other side, happy to have the cool wind airing out his armpits. He didn't want to stink up the vet clinic.

Charlie peeled off Saddlehorn and rolled into the clinic parking lot, careful not to brake too hard and risk a high-speed skid on the gravel. It looked busy. Dr. Anderton's truck and three cars were parked by the front door. Beside it, a tiny woman was trying to coax a snow-white Great Dane, who probably outweighed her by fifty pounds, out of her SUV. The Great Dane wasn't budging.

And then he saw Buster's kennel, just as he had known it would be. Empty.

He looked more closely. The water dish was full, and the food bowl was filled with kibble. He looked at the gate. The padlock was securely fastened. He scratched his head. It wasn't like a Labrador Retriever to leave kibble in a bowl.

He pulled open the back door, hung his backpack on the hook, and headed to the sink to wash his hands.

Megan rushed by as he was reaching for a paper

towel. "Keep your jacket on," she said. "We have another spaying clinic today. The SPCA truck will be here in about two minutes."

Dr. Anderton emerged from the surgical room, pulling off a pair of latex gloves. His brows knitted together when he saw Charlie. "Just the person I wanted to see," he said. "Do you know where Buster is?"

"What do you mean?" Charlie asked. "I brought him back yesterday."

"Well, it's the strangest thing." Dr. A leaned up against the door frame, studying Charlie. "The Bairds didn't get their dog after all."

Charlie's heart began to hammer in his chest. They'd changed their minds.

"No." Dr. Anderton squinted, like he was trying to figure out a puzzle. "They pulled up about a minute after I got here this morning. Right on time, just like we'd arranged."

"Uh-huh," Charlie said, hanging on every word.

"They came in through the front, and they followed me out back."

"Uh-huh," Charlie said again, barely able to breathe.

"And, no Buster." Dr. Anderton narrowed his eyes,

and looked at Charlie with an unflinching gaze. "The kennel was locked. His kibble was untouched. I actually opened the gate and went inside, so I could look right into the doghouse, but I knew he wasn't in it."

"Oh," Charlie said and swallowed.

"I actually thought this might have something to do with you." Dr. Anderton studied Charlie another minute. "But I can see you're as mystified as I am."

The cowbell clanged out front, and a shrill yapping shattered the silence that followed Dr. Anderton's words.

Dr. Anderton cast a quick glance up at the schedule on the whiteboard, and hurried off.

Charlie tried to make sense of what he'd heard. Buster's leash was still on the hook beside the back door, so no one had taken him for a walk. He pushed the door open and walked back over to the kennel.

He measured the length and width with his eyes. He looked up and down at the height of the chain link.

He thought about the pen he and Mark had built for Buster at the back of the house, and how easily Buster had been able to get out of that.

Yes. It was possible. Buster didn't need a long runway to get airborne.

Charlie scanned the empty kennel, and thought about how Buster had arrived at Dr. Anderton's, the very same day Charlie had started to volunteer at the clinic.

He had been Charlie's special responsibility, right from the start.

Together they'd rescued Jayden, at the exact moment he'd needed it.

They'd rescued Tyler, just in the nick of time.

And they'd helped the family in the forest, right before they completely ran out of food for the baby.

Charlie leaned his forehead against the chain link, the rough metal icy cold against his skin.

A light was coming on in his brain. There was one other person Buster had rescued. A person whose dad had split up from his mom and moved away. A person who'd felt so terrible about it all, he'd quit soccer, and stopped doing his homework, and felt bad about everything.

Until Buster.

Charlie turned at the rumble of an approaching truck, in time to watch the SPCA van crunch over the gravel and pull up at the side of the clinic. He waited, while the driver and her helper opened the double doors at the rear of the van.

He cast one more glance at the empty kennel. He scanned the sky, low in the horizon, faintly hoping to see the outline of a super large Chocolate Labrador Retriever, silhouetted against the pale ghost of a sun, shining behind the clouds. And suddenly he understood.

Buster's work here was done.

Yesterday, when it had been time to take him back to Dr. Anderton, Buster had been ready to go.

It was as plain as day. Buster couldn't go to the Bairds. Even if they had a farm and lots of animals, and they would love him just the way Dr. Anderton had said they would, he couldn't go with them.

Buster had more work to do, and he'd gone on to do it.

Charlie blew out his breath, suddenly aware he'd been holding it. Then he started to stride toward the back of the SPCA van.

He had work to do, too.

Chapter 39

PUPPY LOVE

Charlie's shift at the clinic was practically over by the time Megan handed him the last puppy, a pudgy, dark brown, sleepy bundle. The fur across her back had a slight curl to it. Her tummy was still baby pink.

Charlie wrapped the puppy in a warm towel, and started to put her into her carry kennel.

But the puppy opened her eyes and gazed right up into Charlie's. She was the only puppy of eight to open her eyes. Charlie stood, paralyzed.

Megan looked on. "What a little sweetie," she said. "Check that out, Charlie, she's looking right at you. She loves you."

Charlie could hardly form the words. "Is she a Labrador, do you think? She kind of looks like a Labrador."

"Maybe partly," Megan said. "The SPCA doesn't usually get purebreds. She's probably a mix, some

Labrador, some Poodle, and some who-knows-what." She stroked the curls along the puppy's back. "Yeah. Definitely some Poodle." She turned to Charlie. "Poodles are really smart dogs, you know. A Poodle-Lab mix would make a great pet." She started back to the operating room. "And they're hypoallergenic."

Charlie's heart skipped a beat. He tucked the puppy into her kennel, careful to adjust the cone collar so it didn't pinch. He stroked her back, until she settled into her towel and curled up to sleep.

Then he carried her out to the SPCA van, where the driver was securing the last of the kennels in the back.

Charlie cleared his throat. "Hello." He cleared his throat again. "I'd like to adopt one of the puppies," he said. "This one. The Lab-Poodle-cross."

The driver reached to take the kennel from Charlie. "That would be my choice, too," she said. "You come and see us tomorrow, and we'll see what we can do."

Charlie shivered. "She won't get adopted before I get there after school tomorrow, will she?"

"This one?" the driver said. "Look at her."

The puppy had opened her eyes, still puppy blue, dark and serious in the late afternoon light.

"She's obviously in love. She'll be waiting for you."

Charlie stood, watching the truck roll out of the parking lot. Then he scanned the horizon for any sign of movement. He took a deep breath, glanced one last time at the empty kennel, and pulled open the back door of the clinic. He needed to get going. He had a lot to do before tomorrow.

ACKNOWLEDGMENTS

It seems to me that, for years and years, I have read the acknowledgments writers include in their published works, and thought how exciting it would be to salute the people who played an important role in a story's journey, from wobbly idea to actual book. Now that I'm thinking about the acknowledgments for *Rescue*, I realize that I couldn't begin to name all the people who have encouraged me along the way. It seems that when you tell people you are trying to write, they recognize that it is a grand enterprise, one that a writer does alone, for the pure joy of it. So, thank you to all of my friends and family who continued to ask how it was going, and whether I'd heard back from a publisher. Your enthusiasm and interest kept me going back to the keyboard and buoyed my confidence.

On the writing front, I owe a real debt of gratitude

to Maggie and Jenny, my keen-eyed, exacting, supportive, and knowledgeable writing partners. I so appreciate your patience as you critiqued the book, chapter by chapter. I am also grateful for the work of Beverley Brenna at Red Deer Press. The questions you posed for me to think about, your attention to detail and meticulous editing, all combined with your warm encouragement, made the final stages of writing *Rescue* a wonderful experience.

On the home front, my love and gratitude to my two boys, Adrian and Alexander, for your excitement about, and encouragement of, my writing, and of course, all the raw material you provided for me to draw on! And finally, thank you Charlie, for being such a supportive husband, for all your encouragement and confidence building, and for not listening to jazz while I was trying to concentrate on the writing.

INTERVIEW WITH MARIE ETCHELL

You have developed a wonderful character here in Buster. How were you able to create such a believable canine, and was flying part of his skillset from the very first draft of this book?

My family has lived with two Chocolate Labrador Retrievers for a combined total of 25 years. Both were named Ruff, but their personalities were as different as could be. The first Ruff was a handful. He chewed through my seatbelt once while I was driving, ate my mother's shoes, all except for the heels, as we were eating dinner, alienated the neighbours by stealing their children's toys, and generally misbehaved. The second Ruff was better behaved, and only growled if you asked him to get down off the couch. But we loved both dogs. Buster is a composite of their two personalities. And yes, he could fly from the moment I met him!

In this story, Charlie comes to terms with his parents' separation. What made you want to pose this challenge for Charlie and his family? Do you think that books for this age group serve an important role in presenting situations from real life, showing experiences that real children face?

I've been a teacher for a long time, and if there is one thing I've learned, it's that every child is different, every family is different, and every child is dealing with something. I wanted Charlie to come across as a child every reader would recognize, a child trying to make sense of the way his world is changing. I wanted readers to notice that, although his parents' separating makes Charlie both sad and angry, he begins to recognize that life goes on, in spite of the changes. He also learns that he has a role to play in making the new reality work. He has agency. He is a part of making things better.

Rescue contains situations that seem very real, blended with magic. What role do you think magic realism has in helping readers think about their own lives? What role did the magic play in this story in terms of Charlie—how did Buster actually *rescue* Charlie?

The magic in this story serves two purposes. First, what child has not thought about being able to fly, and of having magical powers their parents don't know about, or having a powerful secret? So, first and foremost, the magic provides an opportunity for the reader's imagination to run wild at the thought of all these possibilities. But the magic also serves a second purpose. Buster's ability to fly, and his sixth sense about where he is needed, lead Charlie to people who are struggling. In this way, Buster rescues Charlie from thinking he is alone in his sadness. He is reminded that lots of folks have problems. He learns empathy for the suffering of others, and begins to understand that he can reach out to help, and when he does, he feels better himself.

Your story presents a very realistic description of a vet clinic. What research did you do, in order to make sure aspects of Dr. Anderton's veterinary practice rang true?
I'm not sure if I would call it research! I would call it first-hand experience. Our two Labrador Retrievers had many visits to the vet over the years. Our first Ruff had the emergency surgery that the German Shepherd in the book undergoes. Ruff had eaten the shoelaces out

of several pairs of runners, as well as the fibre from a mat he had unravelled! At that time, we had the most wonderful country vet, who pulled both our dogs through a number of serious situations. Although our dogs were always nervous about going to the vet's, and especially didn't like getting weighed, I always felt we were so lucky to have found such a dedicated, capable, and caring vet.

Buster and Charlie save a lost little boy, support an older kid named Tyler, help catch a gang of smugglers, and assist a homeless family living rough in a clearing between Canada and the United States. How did you come up with this series of adventures? Were there other adventures you thought of? How did you choose the situations into which Buster led his human companion?

The adventures that Charlie and Buster encounter all take place in rural Langley, where my family lived for many years. My sons both played soccer near the field where Buster leads Charlie to Tyler. We often rode our bikes along Zero Avenue, which parallels the Canada–U.S. border. It is a rather spooky road with very little traffic. The border markers—the obelisks that help Charlie identify exactly where the homeless family is sheltering—have always intrigued me. The border between the two countries is the longest undefended border in the world, and it just naturally captured my imagination. Finally, the Salmon River, where Charlie finds Jayden, was a favourite place to walk and explore. I think the adventures Charlie experiences were inspired by the geography of the place where we lived and raised both kids and dogs. As far as other adventures go, I do think about how much I would enjoy following Buster into another rescue mission!

Is there anything else you'd like our readers to know here about your writing process?

The idea for a story comes to me when I least expect it to, and often when I'm riding my bike. I pay attention to the idea for a while, and let it percolate in my brain. But after that, I need to make a plan. Near where I currently live in Victoria, there is a rocky beach overlooking the Strait of Juan de Fuca. If it's not raining, I like to go there with pen and paper, find a rock to perch on, and start a mind map for the story I'm thinking about. I start to write chapters, once I have quite a clear idea for the arc of the story. And much further along in the process, I bring my story, chapter by chapter, to Maggie and Jenny, my long-suffering, patient, and sharp-eyed writing partners. That's when the really exacting work begins.

Did you enjoy writing when you were a child? What advice do you have for young writers who might be reading this book?

My advice to young writers is to read as many books as you can. As I look back on my childhood, I realize how lucky I was to have had parents who read to me. The first book I remember my mom reading to me was a biography of Marie Curie, the woman who discovered the radioactive properties of radium. My mom set the bar very high in terms of the kinds of books we read. In that way, I was exposed to a wealth of ideas and language at an early age. She also encouraged me to use the library. Saturdays meant riding my bike to the library, and coming home with a basket full of books, and the general rule was, if I was reading, I didn't have to do chores. And yes, I loved to write as a kid. I particularly remember writing a very long "novel," called *The Mystery of the Crystal Staircase*. That would have been in my Nancy Drew phase, and, oh, how I wish I could read it now!

Thank you, Marie Etchell, for writing *Rescue*, and for your responses here!